MENACE OF
THE SAUCERS

BOOKS BY EANDO BINDER

Adam Link, Robot
Anton York, Immortal
The Double Man
The Eando Binder MEGAPACK®
Enslaved Brains
The Forgotten Colony
The Impossible World
The Mind from Outer Space

THE SAUCER SERIES

Menace of the Saucers
Night of the Saucers

MENACE OF THE SAUCERS

EANDO BINDER

WILDSIDE PRESS

CHAPTER 1

Thane Smith's rented summer cabin gave him the peace and quiet he needed for his free-lance writing jobs. Only thirty feet beyond lay a grove of tall pines.

Thane walked into their cool shade out of the hot sun. At his favorite reading spot, he sat down with his back to a tree. A scented pine breeze cooled him delightfully. With a sigh of contented relaxation he opened the book.

In the opening lines of the book about Unidentified Flying Objects was a definition: "Flying saucers are more properly called UFO's, or Unidentified Flying Objects…"

"Unmitigated Fanciful Optics," grinned Thane, supplying his own definition.

The book went on to make the brash statement, without a quiver of a doubt, that UFOs had been spied on earth for centuries.

The punch lines came along faster and more hilariously.

Captain Robert Mantell in 1949 had chased a 'saucer' over 20,000 feet, to come down as a mass of wreckage. "The Air Force's claim that Mantell mistook Venus, in the daytime, for a UFO," said the author pompously, "is untenable, for the object had been first detected by radar. Also Mantell had radioed at the last moment that the object was *tremendous*…."

Thane, the skeptic, grunted. Naturally, an oxygen-starved pilot, his brain functioning wildly, would see delusions just before he blacked out. As for radar, the Air Force had plainly called it an 'anomaly'—false image propagation.

Thane started. Out of the corner of his eye, swiftly streaking between two trees for a brief moment, he thought he saw something that flashed in the sun. Something round…moving at fantastic speed…glinting metallic….

"Damn!" said Thane aloud. The book was getting him. But he wasn't going to jump up and rush to the edge of the grove for a better look. A darting hawk…distant jet…maybe some kid's toy rocket…that was all he would see.

Shaking his head, Thane settled back and opened the book again, defying its hypnotic powers.

One of the greatest 'flaps' in UFO history now came up—the notorious 'Washington attack' of July 1952, when some of 67 UFO's had seemingly swarmed over the city. But they had been officially disposed of by the Air Force as due to an 'inversion'—two layers of warm and cold air that refracted ground images into the sky, even creating 'angels' on radar that at first fooled radar-men, not to mention various jet pilots who went up to 'chase' the glowing objects away.

But the stubborn writer claimed it was a cover-up by the Air Force since weather records for that date proved there could not have been a temperature inversion.

The implication, all through the book, was that faced with a gigantic scientific problem far beyond its scope, the bewildered Air Force investigators had never recognized the truth—that flying saucers were not myths but machines, flying with impunity in our airspace and making fools of all pursuing jet pilots. These out-of-this-world craft were blithely credited to an advanced 'supertechnology' on some other inhabited planet in outer space.

The book, in its general review of the UFO phenomena, then listed the 'characteristics' of flying saucers that were repeatedly reported. They often flew at blazing supersonic speeds up to an estimated 5000 mph in ghostly silence. They could turn at right angles without the slightest slowing down. They could stop in one shuddering instant. While hovering in the air, they often 'rocked' back and forth gently, like a boat riding the waves. A glow often surrounded them, best seen at night, that kept changing color and included all the hues of the rainbow—orange, yellow, red, blue, green, white. They…

Thane jerked around. Again, out of the corner of his eye, he had glimpsed something streaking between the trees ahead. This time, annoyed, he put down the book and arose. Just out of curiosity, he had to find out what it was.

Reaching the edge of the grove of pines, he had a clear view of the sky to the north. He squinted. High up was a shiny speck that zigzagged back and forth for a moment, then darted straight down.

Thane caught his breath. The object rapidly enlarged into a clear-cut shape…of *two pie-plates stuck together*.

It dived at supersonic speed…w*ithout a sound*.

It suddenly made a 100 degree turn, level with the ground… w*ithout slowing down*.

Thane gasped, as it streaked almost straight over him about 1000 feet high…a*nd came to an abrupt stop in midair*.

It hovered there…r*ocking gently*.

Thane could now detect a faint glow around it…t*hat changed from orange to blue to white* against the blue sky backdrop.

Thane broke from a gaping trance and ran back through the grove. He didn't believe his eyes or trust his senses. Only one thing could prove he had seen what he thought he saw. He dashed into his cabin and snatched up his instamatic camera, also his movie camera, both loaded.

Would the object be gone in those 10 seconds it had taken him to race back and forth? But when he reached the grove's edge, the strange object was still there, rocking in a slow rhythm.

Panting and fumbling nervously, Thane finally aimed his Kodak and snapped the release. Wanting to get at least one good picture, Thane methodically used up what was left of the roll, seven shots.

While he took them, fevered thoughts piled up in his mind. If the photos, when developed, came out blank—then what? Was he suffering a vivid delusion?

And if the photos were not blank—what *then*? That was even more of a shocking thought. As he snapped the last picture, Thane flicked his eyes up at movement. The flying saucer had suddenly shot forward. It did not get up speed in rising acceleration. It simply went to supersonic speed from dead zero.

Thane sensed something to the north and swung his eyes. He almost staggered. Not one but *two* UFO's. The second one catapulted up from behind a hill, as if it had previously landed on the ground.

It was a different shape, a disk with a dome on top, of a dark flat color like ashes. It arrowed straight up as if striving to reach high altitude before the first UFO could intercept it.

Intercept?

Thane stiffened, sensing that he was about to witness something never before reported in saucer sightings that he knew of. Then, with a grunt, he swung up his movie camera. No still camera could catch what was to come.

The two UFO's seemed to be on a direct collision course, one shooting upward, the other horizontally. Sighting through his viewfinder, Thane winced, expecting the crash. Instead, the two craft incredibly veered apart, then began circling each other in impossible loops and twists.

Dogfight sprang into Thane's mind, as he kept the movie camera whirring. They were far enough away to stay within his field of view as their wild gyrations continued.

Now Thane could detect faint beams stabbing back and forth between the two craft. He felt a tingling in the air around him, as if it were electrified. He thought of the fantastic ray-weapons often featured in science-fiction tales.

It all seemed like science-fiction happening before his eyes. He was seeing the same 'illusions' so many others had seen—only these objects were *real*. Of that Thane was dead certain. Yet the utter silence, the incredible maneuvers, the eye-boggling speeds all made it seem unreal.

The end came suddenly, violently, with a thunderclap of sudden sound. The domed disk simply exploded in a vast shower of sparks that quickly faded and vanished.

Atomized? Blown to atoms? Thane shuddered in awe for there seemed to be no debris. The victorious disk dipped in the air, as if in a triumphant salute, then swung upward at such blurring speed that it was gone in three seconds.

Several seconds after that, with an annoyed exclamation, Thane took his finger off the movie camera's button. He was photographing empty blue sky now. But he had about 40 feet of color film of the mind-staggering aerial drama that had taken place.

Turning, Thane saw something glinting a few feet away. It lay on a cushion of pine needles and hence he had not heard any thud. It was a jagged piece of metal, ash-silver in color—the same color as the domed disk. Was it an actual piece of the exploded craft?

Thane picked it up, still hot, turned it over. A piece of metal that came from some faraway world? Could it be? He put it in his pocket and looked around. If other pieces of the UFO had scattered in the woods, they were never to be found.

CHAPTER 2

"We mean it when we say twenty-four-hour developing service," said the camera store proprietor. "You know that, Thane. You can pick up the snaps tomorrow at noon."

Thane turned at the door. "Don't be surprised when you see the snaps, Bert. You won't laugh."

Bert's mouth fell open. Leaving, Thane paused in wondering thought. What would his developed photos and movie film show—something or nothing? He was in a curious state of mind, not at all sure now of what he had seen.

A UFO? Two flying saucers? A dogfight between them? An exploding craft? With each successive thought he gave a mental gasp, and at the end he was shaking his head in disbelief. Impossible... unless his film corroborated what his eyes had seen. Until then, he would simply have to reserve judgment.

Out on the street of Tanglewood, a small town, Thane glanced across at the local police station. Should he report his strange experience? He winced in advance at the reception his story would probably get, wilder than any flying saucer sighting yet reported. Two UFO's had seemingly fought it out in a ferocious air battle. A new one for the books.

Thane decided to play it smart and wait for his pictures. They would have a harder time laughing at him then. Also, he would like to show the peculiar piece of metal in his pocket, if it were analyzed. Thane turned down a side street, to where a sign proclaimed:

YOU-NAME-IT CHEMICAL SHOP
Theodore Jansen

Jansen took the piece of metal Thane handed him and squinted through his spectacles. "Hmmm...light weight, hard surface, high shine…aluminum maybe. No, magnesium maybe…no. Say, what *is* it?"

"That's for you to find out."

Still "hmmming," Jansen turned and led the way to his small lab in the back. He opened a bottle of acid and put a drop on the metal. Then another acid, and another.

He looked up at Thane, wonderingly. "Where did you get this metal?"

"I'll tell you after you analyze it," returned Thane cautiously.

"I'll have to run special tests," said Jansen, gesturing at various analytical instruments such as a second-hand spectroscope. "Take me a day or two, maybe."

"Don't lose it or destroy it, Professor," warned Thane, turning to go. "I'll drop in tomorrow around noon." He added, "For your own guidance, you may find it out-of-this-world."

Jansen watched him go with squinting, puzzled eyes.

* * * *

Passing a newsstand, Thane returned to the everyday world, refusing to think any further regarding his pictures, the metal, or his sighting. He glanced over the magazines for anything interesting to read. Suddenly his eyes swung in shock to the local paper, *The Tanglewood Weekly*. What was that on the front page?

FARMER SIGHTS FLYING SAUCER read the bold-face headline. A sub-head proclaimed—*Third Sighting of UFO's In This Area in Past Month.*

"You gonna pay for that paper, mister?" queried a shrill voice. Turning back with a weak grin, Thane handed over the coins to the newsdealer. Then he swung into the Daisy Diner.

"A western omelette, Gerty," said Thane to the blonde waitress behind the counter. "And heavy on the French fries."

"Yeah, Thane, I know. And ketchup on the side. Say, I read about that test Mars rocket you told me about. Real exciting."

"Yes, Gerty," said Thane shortly, opening his paper and devouring the front-page story. Yesterday, he would have snorted and skipped it. Today, he could hardly wait to read about the farmer s sighting. The report said that farmer Peter S. Standish's barn had been bathed in light coming from a domed saucer. Standish had seen a crimson liquid drip down from the craft onto some stacked cordwood.

A domed saucer, the same kind Thane had seen destroyed, blown to atoms during the aerial battle with the disk. Thane's eyes now switched below to where it listed the names and addresses of two other people who had sighted saucers.

Thane read the details of both reports, then folded up the paper and strode to his parked car. He was one with them now, one of the 'inner circle' who had seen an unexplainable sight in the sky. He could imagine their confused and shocked state of mind.

Thane drove out of town toward where Standish's farm lay, some three miles west. It was 12:30 and Thane hoped to find him at home from his fields for lunchtime.

A woman and three skirt-hanging kids came out as his car drove into the yard.

"Mrs. Standish?" said Thane, "Is your husband in?"

"Yes, but he won't talk to any reporters," she snapped.

"I'm not a reporter, M'am. I'm a…well, I'm a salesman." Saying 'writer' wouldn't sit well with the farmer either, if he was publicity shy.

"Well, you can just git right on going," came a gruff voice. Standish had come out, a beefy farmer with big hands and an unfriendly expression. "We don't want to buy anything."

I'm not selling anything, Mr. Standish," said Thane hastily. "You see, I saw a flying saucer too, like you did, and I thought we could compare notes and…"

"Hold on, young man," said the farmer harshly. "I didn't see any such things as a flying saucer."

"You didn't…?" grunted Thane. "But the paper said…"

"The paper lied, son. You hear me? A pack of lies. I never made no phone call and never saw any kind of flying contraption with red lights."

"You don't have to be afraid to talk to me," essayed Thane smoothly. "I won't repeat a word to anyone else. It's just for my own curiosity…"

"But I never saw any UFO, I tell you," grated Standish, half-angrily.

"You'll swear that?" asked Thane, incredulously.

"Yep."

"The paper invented the whole story?"

"Every word, son. Now I gotta get to work in my fields. Don't honk your horn and scare the goats on your way out."

There was a finality in the dismissal that defeated Thane. He opened his mouth, then closed it. With a baffled shrug, he got back in his car and slowly drove away, looking back at the farmer's figure, now slumped and sitting on the steps. He was an abject, frightened man, kneading his two hands together as if in anguish.

Why did he look so frightened?

* * * *

Jack Todd, lumbermill hand, was more friendly. His big paw shook Thane's hand in greeting. "What can I do for you, sir?"

"It's about that flying saucer you saw."

"Oh." His face fell. His voice was not so friendly as he went on. "Well, yes, I saw one I guess. But it was nothing much. All over in a few moments. Hardly worth talking about."

"You saw two 'hairy dwarfs' get out of the saucer," pursued Thane doggedly. "They looked around a bit, then spied you. They leaped at you with grunting snarls, you reported, and used their clawed hands. Hands with only three fingers. You must still show the marks, since it only happened ten days ago…"

Thane waited expectantly but the lumberman did not roll up his sleeves to show the scars. "Aw, maybe my story was kinda exaggerated," confessed Todd with a false air. "You know, a man gets to talking with a couple beers in him and he fancies up the story, just for fun."

Lying in his teeth. He, too, has lurking fear in his eyes. He's just trying to kid me out of it, to cover up…

"You turned and ran," said Thane, "and the hairy humanoids then jumped in their ship and sped away. They hadn't really hurt you much and…"

"No, but they sure were fixing to," growled Todd, with sudden intensity. "I think they wanted to drag me aboard their ship and take me away. They wanted to…"

Abruptly, Todd broke off and grinned. "Aw, there goes my imagination again. Look pal. It ain't worth talking about. Forget I said anything. I got work to do. So long…"

* * * *

"Howdy," said Mrs. Theda Ranslick. She was a short, rather plump woman, the typical housewife. Her reddish hair, neatly combed, contrasted nicely with her blue-green eyes. Was there fear in those eyes too? Thane wasn't sure yet.

"About that flying saucer you saw, M'am," began Thane.

"Oh." With the word came a sudden frown. "I don't like to talk about it, mister."

"Why not?" asked Thane bluntly, determined to get to the bottom of this unaccountable reluctance of three witnesses to tell of their sightings.

"Because…well, it might be *dangerous*," she said, her eyes glancing up and down the street.

"Dangerous?" echoed Thane, baffled. "Please tell me more."

Her eyes suddenly fastened on him. "Who are you?" she demanded. "You aren't one of…t*hem*?"

"I don't know what you mean, M'am," said Thane, explaining briefly who he was, where he lived, and what he did.

"Oh, yes," said the woman, relieved. "I heard of you, the writer out at Miller's cabin. Listen, come in, Mr. Smith, where we won't be seen. I want to tell *someone*…"

She gave another nervous glance down the street, then opened the door. Thane followed her in and sat down in the stuffed chair she waved at.

"My children are in school," she went on, "so we won't be interrupted. This thing has me worried, you see."

"The sighting?"

"No, not that. What happened *afterward*."

CHAPTER 3

She gulped at the memory, then began. "It was an egg-shaped object bigger than a bus, sailing across the sky. It flashed blue and green colors, then turned bright orange as it suddenly swung down to the ground. I thought it was going to hit the house. I guess I just stood there frozen, too frightened to even scream."

It took her a moment to go on. "Well, then it stopped just as suddenly and settled slowly to the ground, across in the field back of our house. It stopped and hung eight feet off the ground, I'd say. Just hung there, mister."

Her eyes looked at him in appeal, as if afraid of laughter.

"I believe you," said Thane softly. "You see, I saw a saucer myself. Two of them, having a…well, never mind. It's your story I want to hear."

She went on with more spirit, now safe from ridicule.

"Well, I kept watching in a sort of trance, like. I saw a round doorway open up in the bottom of that machine, and three little men floated down to the ground."

"Floated?"

"Yes, like a balloon. They didn't jump down. Floated."

Anti-gravity, did they have that?

"Well," the woman resumed, "I was fit to be tied, I'll tell you. The three little men—if they were men—were no more than three and a half feet tall and dressed in like one-piece silvery suits and a helmet. Almost like astronauts. One of the little men then held up some kind of instrumen. Don't ask me what it was. It made kind of little sparkles in the air, and he turned around and pointed it in several directions. Like he was measuring something."

She shook her head, mystified. "I guess one of the little men then saw me looking out the window. I saw him turn my way, then make a gesture, and the other two quickly ran under their hovering machine and floated back up inside. Then the oval object just shot up into the sky like a meteor going the wrong way, and in seconds it was only a star that soon winked out."

"Did you tell your husband the story?" Thane wanted to know.

"Yes, the next morning. He just laughed and went to work. But I couldn't keep it inside of me so I phoned the paper—*The Tanglewood Weekly*—and told them. They sent their man around. But it was after that that the rest happened…"

Fear sprang into her eyes and the words came out with a rush.

"The next afternoon, when I was home alone, a big black car pulled up and three men stepped out, dressed in black suits. They rang the front doorbell and said they were 'security agents' of the government who were investigating all saucer sightings, so I let them in. They even showed credentials without my asking."

She paused, her mouth open. "Then what happened?" prompted Thane, impatiently.

"Well, you won't believe the rest. As soon as the door closed behind us, the three men in black became very serious and warned me not to talk about my sighting to *anyone else*. Or else I would be in great trouble."

"Did they make any specific threats?"

"Oh, yes." The woman's eyes shone in terror now. "They didn't say it directly maybe, but they hinted that they would have revenge through my husband or even"—her voice broke—"even my children. I guess what they really wanted was the thing I found," the woman was saying.

Thane sat up. "What thing?"

"The next morning, after my husband left for work, I went out in the field where the saucer had landed. And in the grass I found an odd little…well, instrument of some kind, maybe the one that made sparkles."

"So you gave it to them."

"I was scared not to. And now, I'm still afraid," said the woman, wailingly. "Now that I've done what they warned me not to and told you…oh, what will happen to me?"

The fear in her eyes was the same fear Standish and Todd had displayed. So THAT was the reason they had both reneged about telling their stories. They, too, had been visited by the inexplicable men-in-black.

What had happened to Standish's cordwood? Had the men-in-black visited the farmer, threatened him, and 'confiscated' the cordwood with the red stain?

If someone wanted to keep *solid evidence* of the existence of UFO's out of authoritative hands, that might be the way they'd do it, through impersonation and intimidation.

But just who were the men-in-black, exactly? What was their game?

"Is there anything else you know about those three men who threatened you?" asked Thane hopefully. "Could you describe any one of them or point him out if arrested?"

Auburn locks tossed as she shook her head. "They looked sort of…well, average. They were all about the same build. One was lighter-skinned than the other two. Clean-shaven. Neat shirts and ties…pleasant faces…."

Her voice trailed off vaguely. The hardest person to pick out of a crowd was always the 'average man'. Thane shrugged, giving up.

"Then they drove away?"

"Yes, with a last warning that I should keep my mouth shut about anything I had seen the night before."

"Thanks, Mrs. Ranslick," said Thane, getting up. He needed a chance to digest all this. "Now please don't worry because you told me. I'll never give you away. The men-in-black won't know you told me."

Tooling his way back through town to take the road to his shack, Thane swung around a corner—and gasped. A big black car was parked on the street. And with their eyes glued on him penetratingly, three men lounged at the corner.

Three men in black suits….

CHAPTER 4

Thane drove on, thoughts boiling like an overheated pot. Too much had happened this one morning for him to properly evaluate everything. The switchover from a complete UFO-skeptic to a saucer sighter, all in a few hours, was enough in itself to make him dizzy. On top of that had been dumped the three stories of the other witnesses.

Thane drove home in a sort of short-circuited daze, unable to think any more on the subject. It was hopeless to try getting at his typewriter today, so he again picked up the UFO book to read the rest of it. He had been interrupted in the middle by the dogfight between two UFO's.

Four chapters later, his eyes widened.

There it was in front of him, a special report by John Sheel, the author-UFOlogist, who had for years traveled all around the country and interviewed flying saucer witnesses in person.

"Time and again," wrote Sheel, "I came across witnesses who refused to talk out of fear. They claimed mysterious people had visited them and warned them to keep quiet. The intruders had usually demanded some photo or other piece of evidence that might prove UFOs existed. The visitors were sometimes Air Force officers, or FBI agents, even CIA operatives—so they said. But all were *impostors*. For when anybody checked with the Air Force or FBI, no such person was known to them! But most of all, the visitors were black-suited men who arrived in a big black car. You'll hear more of them later. I've called them the MIB's—for 'men-in-black'."

* * * *

Trying to keep his fingers from trembling, Thane tore open the packet of developed Kodak prints. The first was blank except for a vague blotch. The second and third also. But the fourth…

Thane stared, open-mouthed. Sharp and clear was the first saucer that he had snapped, standing out against the blue sky with unmistakable reality. The other three pictures out of the seven were not as good, but even they showed an undeniable flying machine of disk shape, at various angles.

"I saw them too," spoke up Bert in a hoarse whisper. "You told me I'd be surprised. I was." He straightened up. "Now mind you, I still don't believe in flying saucers, in spite of your snaps."

"You think I faked them, Bert?"

"I'm not accusing you of anything," Bert said hastily. He went on stubbornly. "But I just won't believe in 'em, that's all."

The common reaction of most people, according to Sheel's book.

"Will my movies be in tomorrow at noon, Bert?"

"On the button," Bert nodded. "What have you got on *them?*"

"Something nobody could fake," said Thane, going out.

Thane waited at the You-Name-It Chemical Shop while Jansen took care of a customer. Then the chemist shook his head. "I didn't finish my analysis yet, Mr. Smith. Lordy, what kind of metal is it? Out-of-this-world, you called it. What did you mean?"

"Just what I said, Professor." Thane eyed him. "Can you stand a shock, Jansen? It came from a flying saucer."

"I thought so," said Jansen quietly. "Why should I be shocked?"

"You mean you believe in UFOs?" asked Thane incredulously. "Then you must have seen one yourself."

"No," said Jansen. "But I've read enough books and studied enough sightings by others to convince me. Tell me all about yours, Mr. Smith."

Thane obliged and showed Jansen his photos. The chemist whistled. "Your sighting might blow the lid off the whole controversy, especially if I can analyze that metal and prove it wasn't of earthly origin."

"Right," agreed Thane. "I'll be in tomorrow and see if you have any results." He had not told Jansen of the MIB's. He couldn't quite believe in their machinations himself as yet, not without further substantiation.

Thane could not make up his own mind at the moment, not without further study and thought about the entire UFO phenomenon. He would have to read up more and see what evidence, if any, there was for each theory of origin.

Glancing up from his intense scrutiny of the snapshots, Thane was startled to see a face peering in at him, through the luncheonette window. The face of a man dressed in…black! The face almost instantly disappeared. Were they watching him? Did they know he had photos? Had they checked at the camera shop? Thane ate nervously, with these thoughts whirling in his mind. When he came out, he fully expected to see the three MIB's loitering casually at the corner, near their big black car, but nothing was in sight.

Relieved, Thane got into his own car and wheeled out of town. An hour later, back at his cabin, he strode to his typewriter and yanked out the sheet that still had on it the title *COLUMBUS ROCKET TO MARS.*

That was dead, kaput. Thane had no more interest in writing that article. His next article would be about UFO's, if anything. He began typing up the detailed report of his sighting the morning before, fresh and strong in his memory. Every detail stood out vividly, burned into his brain by its very strangeness.

As the UFO book suggested, when writing details, Thane gave every fact or estimate he could. His technically trained mind came in handy here. Speed of original saucer when coming down, about 5000 mph…shape, that of a flattened disk…size, approximately 75 feet in diameter…height during the dogfight; about 3000 feet.

But no sound. The utter silence of both craft, both in flight and while battling, had been the most eerie aspect of all. Even now, Thane marveled how two craft could circle and dart at supersonic bursts of speed without creating the least sound-waves or sonic booms. There was a real mystery, the uncanny propulsion they must use that somehow suspended the laws of physics as understood on earth.

These peripheral thoughts flitted through Thane's mind as he continued with his report. Duration of sighting…

Thane jerked violently at the knock on the door, totally unexpected. He opened the door and gasped. The three men-in-black were there. He hadn't even heard their black car pull up in the driveway.

"Mr. Thane Smith?" said one of the three politely. He was slightly taller than the others. Swiftly, Thane noted that he was lighter-skinned than the other two, tallying with Mrs. Ranslick's description. The same three MIB's. And it was true that their bland faces were 'average,' not unusual in any way.

"Yes, what is it?" Thane replied, guardedly.

"We're from a security agency of the government. We understand you made a sighting…"

"How did you know that?" demanded Thane sharply.

"Oh, we have ways of finding out such things," the spokesman said, smiling knowingly like an FBI agent might. "We also know you have photos of flying saucers, or more properly, UFO's."

"Perhaps I have," snapped Thane. "What about it?"

The three men looked at each other, then: "We want the negatives," came the blunt words.

"You don't get them," returned Thane firmly.

"But you don't understand. For reasons we can't go into, the government does not at this time wish for the public at large to know that the UFO's exist."

"Which government?" Thane said suspiciously.

"Why, our government—yours and ours."

"Show me your credentials," demanded Thane. Without hesitation, the spokesman withdrew a leather folder from his pocket and opened it up. "See? We are from the Security Service of the Board of Space Technology and…"

"A worthless fake," said Thane flatly. "There's no U.S. seal on it. That makes you impostors. Just who *do* you represent?"

The three men were obviously taken aback at being thus suddenly exposed. Then their faces swung toward Thane, as if in reproval. "If you don't give them to us we will take them away from you."

CHAPTER 5

Thane crouched, tensing his body and loosening his muscles, as he had been trained to do in college. Maybe they didn't know he had been the boxing champ there, and also a karate graduate, not to mention some wrestling and judo stints, as well as football and track.

Thane suddenly leaped and jabbed a jolting punch squarely on the leader's chin, with all the power of his 190 pounds behind it. Whirling, he chopped with the heel of his palm at the second man's neck and heard him groan. Both went down, out of action for the time being.

But the third man, obviously trained for action, stepped back in time to avoid the kick that Thane had aimed for his groin. He leaped forward then before Thane could recover and a fist exploded in his face.

Thane staggered back. It had been a powerful blow. He could feel the blood trickling over his lips. The man came at him viciously, fists pounding. But Thane was now warding off the blows.

Suddenly, he lowered his head and took his assailant by surprise, butting him hard in the midsection. Then Thane kept driving his legs as if heading for the goal posts with a football, with his head still down, and drove the man stumblingly backward until he crashed into the log wall of the cabin with a dull thud.

Groggily, he kept his feet but he was out of action too.

"Out," grated Thane. "Out, you scum."

The three men did not seem to want to tackle the blazing-eyed tall man again. Obediently, they staggered out, half-lugging the man who had been felled by the karate blow.

"I could have killed him," hissed Thane. "Remember that, in case you ever think of bothering me again. I could call the police and demand your arrest, except that it would be three witnesses to one and you could lie your way out of it. So get going. And stay out of my sight."

The three MIB's got in their car. Just as it began rolling, the leader stuck his face out the window, still with its bland, almost friendly expression.

"You are a skillful man of action, Mr. Smith. But we advise you, nevertheless, not to show or publish those photos anywhere, nor submit your report of having seen a UFO dogfight. That is a warning."

The car sped away. Dabbing at his nosebleed with a hanky, Thane had a dazed look in his eyes. *How had they known he had seen the saucer dogfight?* They couldn't have seen the movie sequence themselves, and Thane had told no one yet of his incredible sighting, unique among all sightings in the UFO book he had read.

What uncanny way did they have of finding out such things? Who were they in the first place? Were they part of a hidden organization on earth, as John Sheel had maintained? An ancient race whose culture was unknown to the world at large, basically opposed to civilization as we know it?

Thane returned to his typewriter and finished his report. But he had more to do than that, from now on. He had a mission to perform—ferreting out the secret of the mysterious and menacing men-in-black.

* * * *

Driving toward town with his report the next morning, Thane patted his coat's breast pocket. In there lay his negatives. They were too precious now to be left unguarded or even hidden at his cabin. He would have to carry them with him wherever he went. Now to the police with his sighting report, as a good citizen should.

Thane started. In his rear vision mirror there was…a big black car.

So, they were going to try other tactics, following him and… what? Thane found out as he rounded a bend where the roadway at the right skirted a steep slope ending in rock rubble. With a roar, the black car came up behind him and tried to wedge through to the left.

You won't run me off the road. Thane was already swinging left and blocking them off. Their fenders scraped a little but the black car had to withdraw or get squeezed against the rocky rise to the left of the road.

Now Thane stepped on the accelerator. His Corvair was still good for 100 mph plus on the straightaway ahead. But the big black car hung easily on his tail. Though it had an unfamiliar body style, Thane surmised it was some go-go monster like a Cadillac or Imperial.

Thane couldn't hope to win this race and sooner or later they might maneuver him off the road at another bad spot. He tightened his grip on the wheel and a thin smile came across his lips. They didn't know the trick he had learned while hot-rodding in his younger days.

Thane suddenly braked, taking them by surprise, but only enough so that the black car nudged into his rear bumper. However, when the surprised MIB driver also braked, in delayed reaction, that was when Thane swung a little left and braked hard.

This time, the black car's front bumper struck Thane's rear bumper at a sharp angle. The wheel was practically wrenched out of the other driver's hands, as Thane could see in his rear-vision mirror. The black car careened off the road across a broad shallow ditch and kept on, weaving crazily in a bumpy field.

"Have fun," laughed Thane as the black car disappeared in a tall cornfield. The car wouldn't be damaged nor would the men be hurt, but by the time they got back on the road, their quarry would be out of sight. And Thane knew three different routes to town. Let them guess for the rest of the day which one he had taken.

Twice he had foiled them. Thane felt good. But he also felt a bit sick underneath. He began to divine what a grim game they were playing, and how determined they were to muffle him. What would this cat-and-mouse game escalate into, before it was over?

Arriving in town, with the MIB car nowhere in sight, Thane parked across from the police station. Clutching the envelope that held his report, and patting the pictures in his breast pocket, he took a breath and marched in.

* * * *

The desk sergeant slapped down the typed report. Leaning over, he eyed Thane up and down.

"Are you a drinking man, Smith?" His lip was curled.

"Do you beat your wife, Sergeant?" returned Thane in kind.

"Now listen here, you…" began the frowning officer.

"Look at these," interrupted Thane, handing him his photos.

They made no impression on the Sergeant. "Anybody can fake pictures like that, mister," he drawled, tossing them back. "Look, Smith. We've seen dozens of photos like this, of flying saucers, dishpans, hubcaps, and what have you. And that's just what they are."

"But what if some of the photos and stories are true?" argued Thane, feeling as if he were talking to a stone wall.

The Sergeant snorted. "If we believed every report we got, then we'd have swallowed the story a nice elderly gent came in with last month. How a flying saucer landed near his home and people with long golden hair got out. They flew him through space at a million miles a minute and took him to Mars, where he saw a great civilization. He has a message for the people of earth, that we must all live in peace and brotherhood or…"

He broke off, disgustedly.

"But I'm not a contactee," protested Thane. He had read of them in the UFO book, the lunatic fringe of people who had hitched their wagons to a flying star. Most were sincere and harmless, but deluded. They always had a 'message' to get across to their fellow man.

The Sergeant's phone rang. Waiting, Thane debated whether to add verbally his encounter with the three men-in-black. He shook his head to himself. What good would it do? He would surely be a nut in their eyes then.

This was the typical kind of stubborn disbelief all UFO witnesses met, when reporting to the authorities, according to John Sheel's book. And truth to tell, Thane Smith himself would have listened to Thane Smith's story with an amused smile—only 48 hours before.

The Sergeant hung up and turned back. "If you want to file your report for the record, Smith, it's your right."

"No, thanks." Thane turned on his heel, taking his report and photos with him. The police would neither check his sighting nor hunt down the MIB's, not on Thane's unsupported word.

Thane decided to tackle the Air Force, despite its unsavory reputation as the greatest UFO skeptic of all, at least officially. Watching in his rear-vision mirror as he drove away, he saw no big black car trailing him. Had they given up harassing him?

It was 76 miles to Robbins AFB. The gate guard perfunctorily stopped him, then let him through with a pass to Colonel Taggert, who received all UFO reports.

Broad of shoulder and with a dapper mustache, Colonel Taggert was excessively polite. "We are always glad when the citizenry reports an alleged UAO to us."

"You don't use the term flying saucer, do you?" said Thane, feeling him out. "Or even UFO—Unidentified Flying Object."

A pained expression crossed the Colonel's face. "We prefer the term UOA for Unidentified Aerial Object. After all, nobody has really proved they *fly* under their own power."

That was a good start, thought Thane, already kicking himself for coming. The Colonel read his report with practiced eyes. He whistled a bit on the second page and raised his eyes.

"A dogfight between two UAO's, no less," he remarked in tones carefully kept noncommittal. "I must admit this is a new angle we've never heard reported before. Well, no matter. It says you have photos."

Thane handed them over, narrowly watching the Colonel's reaction. He did not even raise an eyebrow as he shuffled through the four prints slowly. But Thane could detect the slightest quiver of his lip as he asked: "We like to check all photos in case they are of any significance. May we have the negatives, sir?"

"No, you may not have the negatives, Colonel," said Thane flatly. He had been warned by Sheel's book that, in too many cases, the Air Force had permanently 'borrowed' negatives, which were never returned to their owners. Or so, at least, it had been alleged and Thane was taking no chances.

The Colonel shrugged. "You can leave your written report. Mr. Smith, if you wish. It will be thoroughly and scientifically analyzed by our experts and sent to the ATIC at Wright AFB for further evaluation."

"Just what do *you* think of the report, Colonel?" Thane knew it was a loaded question but he was curious to hear the officer's verdict, on the spot.

"As you know," said the Colonel carefully, "I've examined literally hundreds of UAO reports sent in. I've become something of an expert in, shall we say, diagnosing them."

He put his fingertips together. "In my opinion, Mr. Smith—mind you, only an opinion—what you saw were two hawks having a fight, perhaps one having invaded the other one's hunting territory, so to speak."

"Hawks?" Thane was staggered, even though he had been somewhat prepared by classic examples of USAF 'explanations' in Sheel's book. Naming them stars that weren't even in the sky at the time. Calling them balloons that strangely went against the wind at supersonic speed. Saying they were the planet Venus at midnight when any school kid knew that Venus always set long before midnight.

But this—two hawks!

"Why didn't I hear their screeches?" Thane demanded, irate now. The Colonel was treating him like a child. "How could they fly 40 degrees of angular distance in seconds, at a speed of 5000 miles per hour? Why were there no legs or claws or heads or beaks to be seen? Why didn't any feathers drop from their battle?"

"My dear sir…"

"And how could one hawk explode into a shower of sparks?"

"Well, now…"

"Lastly," shot back Thane on his way to the door with his report and photos, "did you get eagles on your shoulders, Colonel, for making UFO's—*UFO'S*, I said—into hawks?"

Thane could see that the Colonel's aplomb had been shattered, by the way he angrily bit his lip. But polite to the last, he merely waved and smiled. "We do our best, sir."

CHAPTER 6

If the saucers could overfly the country day and night with impunity, by the thousands, what security was there? Therefore, as a plain matter of policy, the USAF was forced into the position of denying the existence of craft they most likely believed existed.

In a way, one could sympathize with the Air Force's dilemma and perhaps forgive it for its campaign of deception. As long as the UFO's showed no hostility—and they hadn't made any hostile moves for over 20 years—the Air Force was content to let well enough alone and ignore them, officially.

Privately, however, Sheel's book maintained that the USAF avidly followed up sightings and invariably sent jets in chase if UFO's were detected by radar. There was the belief among UFOlogists, too, that the Air Force secretly gave instructions for jet pilots to shoot at UFO's and try to force them down.

Naturally, one captured saucer and America might learn the great secret of its miraculous propulsion system. But this was futile as the UFO's easily outmaneuvered our best jets and no UFO craft had yet been forced down, as far as anyone knew.

The inherent danger of this course had been pointed out by Sheel too. What if the flying saucers fired back, sometime? Or what if, by sheer chance, a UFO was shot down in flames? Would that precipitate hostilities—a war of worlds?

Back in town, Thane regretted the time lost in visiting Robbins AFB. He had almost forgotten his movie film, which should be ready for pick-up.

"It's here," said Bert as he walked in, waving the box. "Listen, Thane. Would you like to see them right away? I'll set up a projector in the back room and run 'em off. Naturally, I'd like to see them myself."

Both men gasped as the film suddenly switched from early footage of Thane's fishing trip to the edge of the pine grove near Thane's cabin, and the sweep of sky to the north. Two UFO's were cavorting through this arena, most often as a blur of speed. But at times they stood out in clear-cut detail—the flat disk and the domed saucer—unmistakably craft not of this world.

Some of the rays that they shot at each other showed up in the film as faint violet or rosy beams. The dogfight went on, the two craft weaving their unearthly paths through the air.

"Lord!" whispered Bert as the grim pageant ended with the domed disk bursting into a Fourth-of-July shower of sparks. He opened the blinds, his face frozen in amazement. "I'm all shook up," he admitted. "But I still don't believe in 'em."

"You're just like the Air Force," said Thane bitterly. "And the police. Those two agencies, and all authorities, will no doubt continue to deny the reality of UFO's. The only way this can ever be brought into the open is through scientists, as John Sheel said." He grinned. "Then even you will believe, Bert."

Thane next went to a corner phone booth and called Theodore Jansen's shop. "I've pinned down what that metal *isn't*," informed Jansen. "It's *not* aluminum, magnesium, beryllium, scandium or any of the other well-known light metals. The Fraunhofer bright-line test gives a puzzling spectrum, as if it has *lithium* in it."

"What's wrong with that?" Thane wanted to know, then bit his tongue, remembering his college chemistry.

"My dear fellow," Jansen was saying witheringly, "Lithium is as soft as soap and can't be alloyed into a structural metal for a flying craft...or can it? Maybe we just don't know how to do it on earth."

"Do you have to make more tests, Professor?"

"Plenty more," said the phone. "Try me tomorrow, Mr. Smith."

Thane hung up thoughtfully. If the piece of UFO metal turned out to be some unheard-of alloy, not known to earthly metallurgy, then he really had something. That, plus his movies and still photos, should be a triple-threat set of proofs that no authority or scientist could brush off.

There was one good way to blast this whole thing wide open—write an article for an illustrated magazine that would show his photos and the best frames from the movies, and the full analysis of the saucer metal. That, plus his own meticulous sighting report, ought to raise a rumpus.

* * * *

The leader of the men-in-black spoke in a monotone. "We have come for your movie film."

"How did you know I made a film?" Thane gasped. "Are you mind readers?"

He had arrived home to find the three inside his cabin.

The leader laughed. Though he gave no signal, his two men began to circle around Thane from either side. They suddenly rushed him with upraised clubs. Thane brought his hands around, gripping a baseball bat. He was too fast for them.

"When will you three goons learn," panted Thane, "that I can take care of myself? Get going. And if you try to sneak back later, you'll find a loaded shotgun resting in my lap as I type out my UFO article for national circulation. Understand?"

Without a word the three MIB's staggered away. Thane watched them head for the bushes where no doubt they had parked their black car. He started and peered closely. Were they now *floating* above the ground, rather than walking?

It was only a fleeting glimpse, then they vanished in the brush. But only a moment later, a disk-like shape with a dome on top shot up out of the woods.

Thane was thunderstruck. What were the men-in-black doing in a flying saucer…*unless they were saucermen?*

CHAPTER 7

"It's lithium," stated Theodore Jansen, the next day at his store.

"But you told me yourself it's soft as soap," protested Thane. He turned over the piece of hard, shiny metal in his hand. "So how can this be lithium?"

"Oh, I forgot to tell you. It's hardened by potassium."

"Professor, if you are making jokes…"

"What they've done is to *subatomically* link the atoms together. Locked their protons and neutrons into a bond so rigid that the two soft metals come out one supremely hard alloy. Harder than any metal known on earth. As for its other remarkable qualities…"

Jansen counted off on his fingers. "Melting point unknown, way beyond my electric furnace. Magnetizes instantly, then de-magnetizes as soon as the coil turns off. Is completely scratch-proof and non-breakable by ordinary forces. Non-brittle in liquid nitrogen down to minus 345 degrees Fahrenheit. This product was made on some world unthinkably superior to earth in science and technology."

"Don't jump to conclusions," said Thane practically. "You're extrapolating too much from one bit of stuff, Professor. But along with my pictures, it makes for mighty strong proof that UFO's are *real*. That's all I hope to prove. Finding out who or what the sauce-rians are will be a tougher job."

Thane was thinking of the men-in-black as he left. Yes, who or what were they? He was dismayingly reminded of them again, on the drive home, when he saw the domed disk that suddenly shot down from the sky like a striking eagle.

They had waylaid him in a lonely stretch of side road, with no farmhouses in sight. And they must know, by reading his mind, that he now carried with him the damning piece of saucer metal, as well as his negatives and movie film. All three items within their reach…

Thane cursed himself for not bringing his shotgun along, as he leaped from the car and raced for the brush. Over his shoulder he saw the UFO hover low as a hatchway opened. The three men-in-black floated down to the ground and started to give chase on foot. Thane sped into a dense growth of scrub hoping to hide. But if they could pick up his thoughts, by telepathy, how could he avoid capture?

Got to sneak to the small bridge, thought Thane desperately, and cut across the field to the lumbermill…lots of men there… I'll be safe…easy does it, through the bushes to the small bridge….

The three MIB's were waiting at the small wooden bridge that crossed the crick. Thane grinned, watching from a hundred yards away. He had fooled them with his *false* thought of getting to the bridge. All the while he had been creeping the other way, toward the gully that led back to the road.

Taking the chance that nobody else was in the saucer, in the air, Thane dashed into his car. The engine started perfectly. He had read in Sheds book that the electromagnetic force did not damage car engines, merely killed them temporarily.

With a roar, the car shot away. Thane thumbed his nose back at the three startled MIB's who turned and ran from the bridge. Swinging off the side road, Thane got on the highway where traffic was heavy and state police cruised by regularly. The saucermen wouldn't dare show their craft to hundreds of pairs of eyes.

There was no further pursuit and Thane pulled off the highway onto his private dirt road. Again he was alone, but the road led through lofty pines that formed a shield overhead so that a car was just about invisible from the air.

Thane reached his cabin safely, ran in, and barricaded the door. Then he picked up his shotgun, checked that it was loaded, and put it across his knees as he typed. He was facing the door and main window. They would have no way of surprising him.

That's what he thought. The next moment, his eyes bugged as he looked up, to see a hole forming in the roof. Not a hole exactly.

The roof was simply turning *transparent*. And above he could see the circular bottom of a saucer.

What kind of weird powers were they using now? Thane's hands went limp. The shotgun slid to the floor. His whole body was paralyzed. Then some invisible force gently seized him and lifted him up through the hole in the roof. Suspended in the air and rising, Thane looked down to see the roof solid again. He had somehow been whisked through solid matter. Things had gone from the incredible to the fantastic.

He was drawn helplessly up into the lower hatchway of the craft and deposited on his feet, whereupon his paralysis abruptly departed.

"All right, you win," he said turning. "When you men-in-black pull superscience stuff like this, what chance have I…?"

He choked. The three figures he faced were not the MIB's.

Two were men and one was a woman, all three dressed in everything but black. Their form-fitting garments were all colors of the rainbow. One man was dark-haired, the other blond. The girl had red hair.

"Who are you?" Thane said, bewildered.

"Your friends," said the dark-haired man, extending a hand for a handshake. "My name is Thalkon."

"Friends?" grunted Thane. "Funny way to show it, yanking me out of my cabin."

"Yes, to keep the Morlians—men-in-black you call them—from capturing you. Look."

Thalkon waved his hand and a large screen hung on the wall swirled with patterns of color that suddenly solidified into a clear picture. The view showed the domed saucer landing near Thane's cabin. Then the three men-in-black floated out; holding tubular weapons.

"They had decided to use blasters on you," informed Thalkon.

Thane watched in horrified fascination as the MIB's oozed through the side wall and dashed in, ready to gun down their quarry. He could not help grinning at the blank look on their faces when they saw the place empty.

"They will think you somehow slipped away," said Thalkon, "not realizing we rescued you."

"What's this all about?" Thane pleaded, half-dizzily.

"We are the enemies of the Morlians," said Thalkon. "We are the Galactic Vigilantes, keeping law and order throughout space."

Thane stood more paralyzed than before. Paralyzed at this sudden overwhelming revelation, like something out of *Alice in Wonderland*. Finally, he recovered and asked: "You mean you sort of patrol all other worlds like a…a state trooper on our highways?"

"That's a good analogy," smiled Thalkon. "Our mission is to guard earth and prevent the Morlians from accomplishing their long-planned coup."

"You mean they want to conquer earth or something like that?"

"No," denied Thalkon. "It is something far different. And more deadly."

"What could be more deadly?" returned Thane blankly. "Let me have it straight."

"That is all we are permitted to tell," said Thalkon. He turned waving. "My companions are Kintor and Miribel."

The red-haired girl smiled warmly and took Thane's hand. "We will make your enforced stay with us as pleasant as possible." With her around, thought Thane, it would be more than pleasant.

"Thank you," she said with a little bow.

Thane's face turned crimson. "Good Lord, you read thoughts too," he stammered, cutting off further thoughts he had about her. Kintor, the other man, put a peculiar skullcap on Thane's head. "It is not fair for your private thoughts to be an open book. And you have not learned to shield your own mind. This psycho-shield will do it for you."

"Thanks," said Thane, relieved. "But where are you taking me?"

"To our mother-ship," the girl replied. She waved her hand at the monitor screen with a brief word of explanation to Thane— 'thought control.' The screen's spangled patterns now solidified into the scene of earth's curvature spinning away from them below.

Thane clutched at a railing, utterly startled. "We're flying in space," he breathed, stunned.

"Just like your astronauts," Miribel nodded. "Our mothership is positioned at a height of 1000 of your earth miles."

She waved again and the scene abruptly switched upward, where a cigar-like object hung in the black sky. It rapidly enlarged as they drew closer until Thane could see its immense size.

"1,000 feet long?" he guessed, knowing he was underestimating.

"Times ten," smiled the girl.

"10,000 feet, two miles?" Thane looked at her disbelievingly. "But Echo I, the balloon satellite that came down in 1968, was only 100 feet wide and at an altitude of 1,000 miles could be seen with the naked eye from earth. Then your 2-mile ship should be easily visible…"

"Only if we choose it to be," said Miribel. "We have methods for bending light-rays, or radar pulses, so that nothing registers on the eyes or instruments of your people."

Now, on the screen, Thane could see a hatchway opening in the mother-ship. But it was not like a trapdoor or any conventional entrance. It was more like the lens opening of a camera, slowly and steadily enlarging into a round hole.

CHAPTER 8

As their craft shot into the entry port of the mothership, Thane was struck by something. "We left earth with enormous speed and now we decelerated at a rate that should have crushed us all with g-forces. Why do we feel nothing?"

"We are isolated from all other gravity forces by an electromagnetic field," spoke up Kintor, who was punching the button controls of their disk. "In this EM field, which simulates gravity, each of us—every atom of our bodies—is pulled along in unison, so that there is no wrenching or strain."

"What happened to the law of inertia?" Thane demanded. "It works independently of gravity."

"We suspend the law of inertia," said Kintor blandly, "but I can't explain how to an earth mind. There are certain things beyond the understanding of your science and for which you have no terms."

Their small craft now stopped, within the giant mother-ship. Through a porthole, Thane could see that they were parked along with a dozen other saucercraft in a row. Thalkon led the way as they stepped out in a huge chamber.

Thalkon and Kintor started floating away. Miribel took Thane's hand and suddenly he too was floating without visible support.

"Mental levitation," explained the girl briefly. Thane let it go at that. But there was one question he could ask.

"What are your plans for me?"

Thalkon turned his head to answer. "We will keep you here as our guest until the Morlians—the three men-in-black—give up waiting for your return to your cabin."

"But just why are they after me and my UFO evidence?"

"Because they don't want the world at large to suspect that they, being aliens, really exist. They want the situation to remain as confused as it is, with the authorities officially denying the existence of UFO's and therefore, of any people from outer space."

"Then that's why they intimidated Standish, Todd and Theda Ranslick, as well as myself," mused Trane.

"And many thousands of others," added Thalkon. "Whenever anyone's sighting carries some strong evidence with it—photos, movies, artifacts—the Morlians move in and hush it up."

"And my sighting was particularly damaging?"

"Exactly, Thane Smith. You happened to witness—and photograph—a battle between two saucers. Namely, between a Vigilante craft and a Morlian ship. And you even obtained a piece of the destroyed Morlian craft."

"You know all that too, eh?" said Thane, uncomfortably. "I feel as if I've been a goldfish in a bowl with my every movement watched for the past four days."

"The hairy dwarfs are allies of the Morlians, from a different world. Now, what you didn't hear from Jack Todd is one important part of his story. When he saw their saucer land and went there to investigate, he first spied them talking to Morlians who had landed nearby in their own saucer. That's what the Morlians had to cover up when they intimidated Jack Todd, as well as the scratches from three-fingered hands."

Thane nodded. "Now what about the non-hairy little men?"

"They were *our* allies," responded Thalkon. "The instrument that sparkled, according to the woman observer, was a device for detecting any landed Morlian ship within twenty five miles. We keep constant vigilance against their landings for a certain reason. What they wanted from the woman was the instrument itself. The Morlians have none themselves. Their technology is behind ours."

Thane realized he was involved in a very complex game that might take hours or days to explain to an earthman. He couldn't hope to encompass the vast scope of this outer space drama and intrigue with a few questions.

"And the Standish sighting?" he asked, just to take care of that. "Whose ally was that, yours or theirs?"

"Neither," said Thalkon, really surprising Thane. "You see, besides the Vigilantes and Morlians, there are many other worlds whose exploration craft occasionally stop at earth. Their intentions are often just scientific observation. But since they inadvertently dropped exhaust fluid that stained some cordwood red, the Morlians felt obliged to cover up that sighting too."

"In other words," summed up Thane, "the Morlians are fanatically determined to keep earth from realizing that UFO's of any kind or origin are real, thus protecting their own secret doings on earth?"

"Exactly," nodded Thalkon. "Wherever strong evidence shows up, they make it their business to suppress it."

"But they've failed in my case, thanks to you Vigilantes," said Thane.

Thalkon eyed him. "We didn't want the Morlians to get your evidence because"—he paused before going on—"we want it ourselves."

"You...what?" choked Thane. "You mean you snatched me away from the Morlians only to get the evidence away from me?"

"Yes, but we never use what you call strong-arm methods. Never force. We can only *request* that you turn it over to us, voluntarily."

"Why?"

"We too wish to remain 'myth' to earth-people. And your evidence is too significant, revealing the struggle going on between the Galactic Vigilantes and the Morlians."

"Please." Thane's mind was whirling now. "I can see the reason for the Morlians wanting to hide their presence, assuming they've got some rotten design on earth. But if you're on our side, as guardians of law and order as you claim, why should *you* conceal your presence?"

Thalkon shook his head rather helplessly and Miribel answered.

"It is not permitted, Thane Smith. We are bound under certain Galactic Laws regarding other civilized worlds. It is doubtful if we could ever really explain and make any sense to you. But we are just as anxious as the Morlians to keep the presence of our saucer-craft on earth a secret."

"Maybe *your* plan is the rotten one," countered Thane, confused and suspicious. "How do I know your motives are good?"

"You don't," admitted Miribel.

"All right, if the Morlians are so wicked, what is their sinister plot against earth?"

"It is not permitted to tell."

Thane got up and threw his hands in the air. "It is not permitted! It is not permitted! So far you've left me completely in the dark and I don't know who or what to believe."

"No matter," spoke up Thalkon. "The question is, will you turn over to us the UFO evidence you carry?"

"And if I refuse?"

"That is your right, Thane Smith. I told you we do not use force. You see, it is not…well, not permitted."

"I'm glad for once to hear that phrase," grinned Thane, without humor. "You mean then that if I choose to keep my evidence, you won't do anything about it. What if I write up this whole experience?"

"You won't be believed," smiled Miribel. "At least, not our rescuing you and hiding you up here in space." She frowned. "However, the story of your sighting, backed up with three kinds of evidence, might stir up a furor and bring about scientific investigation of the saucer controversy on earth."

"Which is what you don't want," guessed Thane.

"Which is what we don't want," agreed Thalkon. "Not yet," he added. "Someday, earth will be told all, but that day has not yet come."

"Crazy," said Thane, pacing the floor. "The whole deal's mad, insane, incomprehensible. Two groups of aliens on earth, one struggling against the other. One with evil intentions, the other beneficent—presumably. And both groups striving to keep their existence unbelieved among earth-people. Wild…nonsensical…."

"On one thing we can agree, though," said Thalkon calmly. "That we keep you here until the Morlians—the MIB's—leave your cabin."

Thane nodded. "I can't argue with that. But let's get things straight. While I'm here, I will not turn over my UFO evidence to you. And I firmly intend to try to prove that saucers exist, when I get back, using that evidence. Okay with you?"

Thalkon sighed and rose. "It is not permitted to interfere with a free man's decisions. Let us see now what is going on at your cabin…"

He waved and a nearby monitor screen lit up, its chaotic colors blocking into a scene inside Thane's cabin.

The place was a turmoil with the three MIB's ransacking the place, searching everywhere.

"Blast them," growled Thane. "Wrecking my place. They think maybe I hid the evidence somewhere."

A moment later, they gave up, staring at each other. Then they went out, floated into the woods, and took off in their domed saucer.

"They've left," said Thane. "But why didn't you just blast their saucer before and free me of their unwelcome attentions?"

"Another squad of three MIB's would have been instantly assigned to go after you and your evidence. We would have gained nothing."

Thane had a curious thought. "Yet one of your saucers shot down a Morlian domed disk, during that aerial dogfight I saw. What was that all about?"

"That Morlian craft," said Thalkon, "was engaged in placing a certain installation in that area, which had to be prevented at all costs."

* * * *

On the trip from the mother-ship back to earth, in the small saucer, Thane found himself staring at Miribel and admiring her. She looked like any girl on earth except for her alien clothing. She could be anyone's sister, or wife…

"Are you people…uh…perfectly human?" Thane asked. "A rather blunt question and I don't mean to be impolite. Do you only *look* human or are you human through and through?"

"We're as human as you," laughed the girl. "Evolution on similar worlds follows the same pattern with the same end result. That's a biological rule your scientists have not yet discovered."

"You'll have to tell me about your world sometime," began Thane. "That is, if we ever meet again."

"Who knows?" said the girl noncommittally. "That is up to chance."

Thane hoped chance would deal the right cards, in the future, so that he might again see this lovely creature from…where? He didn't even know where her home world was. But there was no time for more questions as the saucer landed outside his cabin. It was night now.

"Wear your psycho-shield cap constantly," said Thalkon, "And the Morlians will be unable to trace you by your thoughts."

Miribel waved from the underside hatchway as it slowly closed. Then the disk spun away at fantastic speed. Thane stood staring at the spot for a while. He turned to his cabin.

Hands poised over the keys, he felt momentary guilt. He was, in a sense, betraying his alien rescuers, who hoped he would not write up his sighting or present his gold-plated evidence.

Setting his lips firmly, he began typing. This was not his bare report but a full-blown article aimed at mass circulation. It would go in prestigious *Pictorial* magazine and come to the attention of authorities and scientists. All would know this could be no crackpot presentation.

It might well blow the lid off the UFO controversy and start off serious investigation. It might start the ball rolling to where the National Academy of Science, Congress, even the United Nations became interested and launched a worldwide search for UFO's. Sometimes, it only took a spark like this to set a conflagration going, one that was already overdue according to John Sheel's book.

Thane typed half the night. He even forgot the loaded shotgun within easy reach. Once he heard a suspicious sound outside, but found it was an opossum grubbing through his garbage pail.

The MIB's, mystified by his complete disappearance, had been thrown off the track for now anyway, giving Thane the breathing spell he needed to finish his job. He wore his psycho-shield cap as Thalkon had suggested.

Tomorrow he would deliver the completed manuscript. The title was—SAUCERMEN AMONG US.

CHAPTER 9

He was ushered into the sanctum of *Pictorial* magazine with his briefcase. Bill Eggerton, editor-in-chief, greeted him with a perfunctory smile but then barked: "Listen, Thane. You phone me at the beastly hour of 9:15 when you know no office gets going before 9:30. We're all just waking up. Then you tell me you have a 'hot' thing about a UFO sighting, plus pictures, and that you want it read and okayed today."

"You won't regret the rush treatment when you read this," said Thane, tossing over his manuscript.

"By God, it had better be sensational," growled Eggerton. "You know, it's only your reputation as a top writer that ever got me to shove aside all my other work. And as you know, we've kept shy of the UFO mishmash for fear of catering to contactee kooks. Who is this sighting by?"

"By myself," said Thane quietly.

"You?" exploded Eggerton. "But last time you were here, with that Venus rocket piece, you told me you'd never touch flying saucers with a ten-foot pole."

"I found an 11-foot pole," said Thane humorlessly. "What I said then and what I'm saying now are horses of two different colors."

Eggerton was still shaking his head. "Hard-headed old Thane Smith a saucer sighter. All right, hand over the photos first. If they aren't good, it's a wash-up right away."

Thane handed over the stills. Eggerton scrutinized them carefully. "Not bad. But then I've seen UFO photos just as striking that were faked."

"You have my word that these are authentic," said Thane.

Eagerly now, Eggerton began reading the sheaf of typed papers. He whistled now and then, during the first half. After he finished, he slammed down the manuscript. "Dammit, man, you know we don't use science-fiction."

"Every word is true," said Thane tightly.

Eggerton fixed him with a cynical eye. "I don't know what your game is, Thane, but you don't honestly expect me to publish—or believe—this brainstorm, do you? It can't be true. You dreamed it or drank the wrong rot-gut. You're a victim of illusions, delusions, hallucinations…"

"Skip the psychoanalysis, Bill," snapped Thane. His voice turned soft "It'll sell a million extra copies of *Pictorial*."

"It'll get us a million subscription cancellations, you mean," roared Bill, banging his fist on the desk. "Utter drivel, nonsense. We'd be the laughingstock of the nation."

"I've got movies to back it up, Bill. Better than the stills."

"All UFO movies stink," retorted the editor.

"How about this?" Thane held up the piece of metal. "Analyzed as an alloy of lithium and potassium in an atomically locked state. Superior to any metal on earth. I have the signed statement of a competent chemist."

Eggerton pushed aside his hand. "I don't care what you have. The whole story is ridiculous to begin with. It just doesn't have the ring of truth to it."

"Prove that, Bill," challenged Thane. "Call in some outside person and let him read it. Not one of your editors, who might be as prejudiced as you, but someone not connected with *Pictorial*."

"All right," agreed Bill, snapping on his intercom. To the puzzled receptionist he said: "Miss Blaine. Go out in the corridor and ask the first person who comes along to step into my office. Tell them it's important. I'll explain the rest."

While waiting, Thane mused that all was not lost. If the third party made an objective reading of his manuscript and gave one bit of approval to its matter-of-fact style of presentation, Bill would probably agree then to look at the movies, which should swing him.

"Yes, what is it, sir?" came a feminine voice back of them.

"Oh, it's a *girl* that Miss Blaine rounded up," said Bill.

Thane turned, and nearly fainted. "Miribel," he stammered, "You?"

It was unmistakably the red-headed girl of the Vigilante saucer, only dressed now in earth-style clothing so that no one would suspect she was not of this world.

Her eyes turned on him coldly. "I beg your pardon. My name is Myrna Darby. I was returning from an appointment with my lawyer when a girl asked me to step in here."

"But aboard the saucer where we met..."

"Saucer? What are you talking about? We have never met before—anywhere."

"What are you trying to pull, Thane?" said Bill, eyeing him wonderingly. "You *are* seeing things." To the girl he said: "Please forgive me. I need your help. Will you read this manuscript and tell us whether you believe what it says? I'll pay you for your time."

Though surprised at the unusual request, the girl agreed.

Thane watched her face as she read, especially when she came to the last half describing how he had met Miribel, the saucer girl, and their trip into space.

Not a flicker crossed her face. Not a sign of betrayal of her new pose as an earthgirl. She smiled as she finished. "The way you describe this Miribel, I'm flattered that you mistook me for her."

"But you *are* Miribel," insisted Thane. He went on desperately. "Surely you're not going to make a liar out of me. One word from you and my story is proved...."

Thane choked off. He remembered now Miribel saying, "We are just as anxious as the Morlians to keep the presence of our spacecraft on earth a secret."

"Do you believe what you just read, Miss Darby?" asked Eggerton now.

She shook her head. "If you mean is it convincing, no. I don't believe a word of it. Whoever wrote it must have a vivid imagination. It doesn't have...well, the ring of truth."

Bill Eggerton looked triumphantly at Thane. "Thanks, Miss Darby. Sorry to trouble you. Leave your address with the receptionist and we'll send you a check."

"That won't be necessary. Glad to have been able to help." She went out without a backward glance at Thane, who stood slump-shouldered and defeated.

"Listen, Thane," said Eggerton in a kindly voice. "When you begin to imagine UFO dogfights and rides in saucers, and when you imagine that any strange girl going by is your 'Miribel'…well, why don't you see a doctor, old man?"

Without a word, Thane picked up his pictures and manuscript and left, his face burning. Humiliation and anger both burned in him. He rushed out in the hall. The girl was just getting in the elevator. Thane squeezed in just before the doors closed. They were alone.

"Miribel," accused Thane, bracing himself for a possible slap in the face.

"Yes, Thane?" she said sweetly. "How nice to meet you again."

She touched his arm, sympathetically. "I'm sorry, Thane. It had to be. It is too important. We must remain unknown here on earth."

"But why?"

"For your world's own good," said the girl sincerely. "You must believe me. Someday, perhaps, we will explain why it is not permitted to make ourselves known."

Thane could not remain angry with her, despite what she had done. As they stepped out of the elevator below, Thane asked, "Do you have to rush back to…wherever you hide out? Can you take time to have lunch with me?"

"It's the least I can do to make it up to you," she said, taking his arm.

At a quiet restaurant, Thane stared at her curiously. "I know better than to ask leading questions, Miribel. I'll only get that it-is-not-permitted-to-tell routine. But can you at least tell me something about your home world? Where it is and what it's like?"

"It is permitted to tell that," she laughed. Her face became dreamy. "Our world is a beautiful world. We've had almost a million years of civilization, you see. It is all like one big park or garden. We live in roaming homes that can waft anywhere we wish, via anti-gravity forces."

"What planet is it, of what star?"

"In your earthly terms, it's just one of the many distant stars with numbers—B-Beta-148. It is 787 light-years away, in your earth terms."

"Then you're more than 787 years old, if you traveled here at the speed of light. Or do you use some space-warp or dimensional short cut to travel swiftly across the universe?"

"You've been reading John Sheel," said the girl. "We did too, as we read all earthly books about UFO's and keep tabs on how close they get to the truth. Our method of space travel may be described as teleportation."

"Instantaneous travel?" marveled Thane.

"Yes. Space and time are different than you think, here on earth. You have not discerned the truly basic laws of the universe yet, in which there is an Nth dimension that crosses all points in space at the same place and time."

"Whoa," said Thane, "go slow. You're way over my head already."

"There is no simpler way to describe it. Briefly, we transpose our spaceship into the Nth dimension, then settle down on earth which is close by, as all worlds are. It takes a very intricate chart, however, to find your chosen destination out of so many, all packed together."

"You really travel in one instant across 787 light-years?"

"It does not even take one instant. There is no time in the Nth dimension. It is like de-materializing on our world and then materializing on earth, at the same time."

Thane nodded. That was like so many sightings listed in Sheel's book, where the UFO seemed to suddenly appear in a hazy mist, out of nowhere. Also, many saucers seemed to *fade* away instead of flying away. It tied up one loose end of the UFO riddle, if nothing else.

"What do you think of earth?" asked Thane, curiously, expecting a reaction of disdain or worse, in comparison to her far-advanced world.

Surprisingly, Miribel said: "I like earth very much. The people are warm inside. Good stock, as planetary races go. And it's amusing, really, how provincial earth-people are, resisting the belief that there are countless other worlds in space superior in science, technology, culture, and social progress."

"I guess we're sort of arrogant," Thane agreed humbly, ashamed at how 'provincial' he had been only five days before.

"It's just that your civilization is so young," said Miribel soothingly. "You have barely emerged from prehistoric savagery in the past 10,000 years. That is a mere tick in the time of planetary evolution. In a few thousand more years you will be a mature member of the United Worlds."

"United Worlds?" Thane was intrigued. "What's that?"

"A galactic organization of advanced worlds…" The girl put a hand to her mouth. "But it is not permitted to tell more."

Thane groaned. It was exasperating to get a hint of so many vast new revelations out in the macro-universe only to have all further illumination cut off abruptly.

"I like your earth food too," volunteered Miribel, digging into a dish of Moo Goo Gai Penn with relish. "Spicy, strong, carelessly cooked, but it has a vigorous quality."

"Everything we do is backward?" winced Thane.

She turned her limpid, indigo eyes on him in quick understanding. "Don't feel so bad. After all, the child has to grow into the man. The human race will gain wisdom in time…hopefully."

"You mean—?"

"Not all races, humanoid or otherwise, develop in the right way. The wrong twists and turns in their history and they become maverick worlds, like Morli."

"The men-in-black?"

"Yes, their world pursues its own evil ends, as do many other wayward planets. Remember, out of millions of civilized worlds they cannot all follow the right path toward a morally matured society. That is why the Galactic Vigilantes were formed."

"I'll ask no more," grunted Thane. "Verboten."

After paying, Thane strolled out with the girl. "I'm heading back for Kennedy Airport," he said. "And you?"

"Oh, I'll just wander around the city until dark, when I'll be picked up by a scout saucer."

"Want to join me in a taxi ride to the airport?"

She agreed and Thane hailed a cab. After they stepped in, the girl suddenly tensed. "I feel danger," she said. "Close by...the driver! He's a Morlian!"

A bland, 'average' face turned and grinned mockingly at them. In his hand was a tubular device from which a violet mist belched, straight into their faces.

"Sleep gas," gasped Miribel. That was the last thing Thane heard as his mind plunged into a black pit.

CHAPTER 10

When Thane's mind struggled awake, he saw clouds rushing by at a dizzying rate. He was in a plastic bubble dome on top of a wide flat saucercraft.

"A Morlian craft," came Miribel's voice beside him. She had already come to. Across the chamber were three Morlians, manipulating button controls. Miribel pointed down. Thane saw endless waters rushing beneath. "The Pacific Ocean," she continued. "And I have a hunch…"

Suddenly, the craft tilted downward. "We're going to crash at sea!" gasped Thane in alarm.

But to his surprise, he felt no jar as they contacted the watery surface. Instead, the saucer slid smoothly under the waves and simply continued.

"All saucercraft can submerge and sail down through the ocean," said Miribel casually. "It makes no difference to an electromagnetic propulsion engine." Thane recalled now that Sheel's book had listed sightings of 'diving saucers' many times.

"How far down are we going?" wondered Thane as the light died and a powerful searchlight beam stabbed ahead.

"Perhaps to the bottom," shrugged Miribel.

Thane blinked. "Five to seven miles down, without trouble?"

"This plasto-dome and the craft's hull are impervious to any pressure," nodded Miribel. "Morlian saucer technology is close to ours. We are perfectly safe. But at least I've learned something. The Morlians have one base at the sea bottom, here on earth."

She pointed down and Thane saw a glow of light that grew into a huge plasto-dome resting on the oozy ocean floor. As the saucer tilted and dived at breakneck speed straight toward the dome, no door or hatchway of any kind opened. Though turning pale, Thane said nothing this time.

There was a peculiar sensation for a moment, as of strings vibrating without sound, and the next micro-instant the saucer was inside the dome, coming to a neat landing on a platform.

"How was that miracle performed?" asked Thane weakly.

"They simply changed the vibrational rate of the whole craft and oozed through the shell of the dome. The saucer, in effect, had become a cohesive mass of X-rays which simply penetrated through the domes solid material. Clear?"

"As mud," responded Thane. "I'll take your word for it, since we're safely inside the dome. It's aerated, I suppose?"

It was, for they were ushered out into breathable air, within the dome. The Morlians nudged them onto a square platform which then floated free and gravitated to the door of a square chamber within the dome.

"Highman ZX-22 wishes to see you," said one of their captors.

"Highman means leader or commander of this dome," explained Miribel. "And the Morlians have no names, by the way, only numbers."

"Are they perfectly human?"

Miribel nodded. "Perhaps more perfect than we are, for all Morlians look alike, at least to our eyes. There are only slight differences in complexion or size, but otherwise they are millions of peas from the same pod."

"Weird," said Thane, seeing that Highman ZX-22, before whom they stood, looked quite like the average man too.

The Morlian commander glanced up from a small desk, smiling in a fatherly manner. "We have captured two prizes," he stated. "One of the top Vigilante agents, and the earthman whose sighting we had to suppress. You are both dangerous to us. Yes, this is one of our many secret bases on earth," the Highman continued. "But you, girl Vigilante, will never return to reveal it."

He said it almost jovially, despite the chilling threat.

Miribel said nothing, only paling a bit.

The Morlian fixed his eye on Thane. Only there in its depths lurked a hint of ruthlessness. "You, earthman, will be easily brain-altered. What is the earth term? Oh, yes…brainwashed. Then you will be an aid to us, instead of a hindrance. That is all," finished the Highman. "Take them away."

The other Morlians separated them, prodding Thane onto a square float-platform, while Miribel was led the other way.

She turned her face and suddenly, silent words leaped into Thane's mind. "Thane! I'm using a closed telepathy beam so the Morlians cannot hear me. Do not give up hope. The Vigilante forces will scour the world for us. They'll find us…if we're lucky."

With a last brave '*au revoir*' from her indigo eyes, she turned away.

Thane's float-platform, plus one Morlian guard, wafted across the dome to another chamber. Within, a Morlian in a white jacket, as indistinguishable as the others, stood up.

"Brainwash Thane Smith, UQ-77," said the guard, leaving.

Thane's sinking feelings sank even lower. What could he do? Here he was isolated in a sea dome miles down in the lightless ocean depths. Nobody on earth knew of his trouble. Nor would it do any good if they did. Probably even the Galactic Vigilantes had no clues to go by.

This 'brainwashing'—what would it do to him?

Thane suddenly panicked. As UQ-77 came toward him, Thane lashed out with his fingers, held stiff, poking them violently into the Morlian's throat. He gagged and staggered back at this judo trick.

Thane ran out and kept running until he came to the edge of the undersea dome's shell. Panting, he turned like a trapped rat.

The Morlian, now recovered, came floating toward him. "That was foolish, earthman," he said like a father reproving a child. "Where do you hope to go?"

Thane slumped. Even if he somehow broke through the dome shell he would meet the enormous pressures of sea bottom waters that would crush him flat in an instant, even before he had time to drown.

Escape was a meaningless word, here in the dome.

Thane allowed himself to be led back, docilely. This time, the Morlian aimed a tubular device at him. A brief whine and Thane felt himself paralyzed, standing stiffly and unable to move a muscle.

"That's better," said UQ-77, rubbing his hands. "Now we will place this over your head...so." It was a metallic bucket helmet. Then the Morlian stepped back and shot another ray at the helmet. Thane felt his voluntary senses slipping, sliding, falling down a steep slope into a dreamy pool.

"That places you in a hypnotic state," informed UQ-77 in conversational terms. He went on like a dentist soothing his patient: "Now this won't hurt, as a hypno-beam carries my commands into the cerebellum centers of your brain."

True, Thane felt no pain or discomfort. The Morlians were not deliberately cruel, merely accomplishing their ends in the most efficient way.

"It's all over," said UQ-77, taking off the helmet. Like any earth hypnotist, he then snapped his fingers in Thane's face. Thane became conscious with a start, his mind slowly gearing itself to normal.

"Do you believe in flying saucers?" asked the Morlian.

"Don't be an ass," retorted Thane with vehement conviction. "Anyone who believes in that rot is a kook."

"Kook? Oh yes, idiot," nodded UQ-77. "Now, Thane Smith, were you ever in a sea bottom dome, the prisoner of Morlians?"

"Who or what are Morlians?" said Thane, puzzled.

"Do you know the name Miribel?"

"Sounds nice but I never met the chick."

"Good," said the Morlian, rubbing his hands again. He spoke into a microphone. "The prisoner is prepared for return. He will remember nothing of his trip back to the upper world."

* * * *

He glanced at the four photos he had wanted to submit with the article to *Pictorial* magazine. They showed only indefinite blurs in the sky to his hypnotized eyes. He held a strip of movie film up to the light. It showed two hawks fighting. He picked up the piece of metal, plainly part of a tin can.

"Funny I should think I had evidence of UFO's," he murmured, shaking his head. Then, following the silent series of programmed commands placed hypnotically in his brain, he dumped them into the trash basket and remembered they had been given to him by three persons—Peter Standish the farmer, Jack Todd at his lumbermill, and Theda Ranslick the housewife.

Purposefully, he sat down at his typewriter. "UFO's exist," he wrote rapidly, "in sick brains. Three people came to me in the past few days, excitedly handing me so-called evidence of flying saucers. Their still photos, color movies, and a piece of an exploded UFO are all not only obvious but pitiful fakes. Suffering from delusions, they typify all saucer sighters—every one…"

His keys clacked away steadily, as he wrote more and more scathing words about the mind-lame people who claimed to have seen unknown flying objects and queer little humanoids. And the three items of 'proof' he had been offered—he would keep the donors anonymous for their own sake—would prove only that misguided people had created the entire UFO mythology.

It was by-lined Thane Smith, a respected name. Printed in some national magazine, it would convince thousands, even millions, of wavering people that besides Santa Claus, there were no flying saucers. He was doing his part in preventing a whole nation from being deceived by a purely psychological phenomenon. The sooner that was straightened out, the better off America would be. Logic, objectivity, common sense had all been marshaled devastatingly to blast the mythical UFO's right out of the sky—forever.

And Thane would accept no pay. It was a public service.

Thane's car was on its way to the airport when the UFO appeared. It was a silvery disk of the Galactic Vigilantes. Thane glanced at it, without surprise.

A gull, he said to himself with full conviction. The hypnosis of the Morlians had done a thorough job.

Thane did not even believe it when the saucer hovered overhead, matching his speed, and a purling beam of energy lifted the entire car into the air. A hatchway opened underneath and the car vanished within.

Then the silver saucer tilted and shot straight upward. There had been no witnesses.

Not even Thane. He looked at Thalkon blankly, without recognition. When the saucer catapulted high into space, he looked up at the enlarging mother-ship and then away, unconcerned, unaware. Anything relating to flying saucers simply could not penetrate the hypnotic spell and register on his mind.

"A bad case," murmured Thalkon to Kintor, who was at the controls of the disk ship. "Can we succeed in de-hypnotizing him?"

After entry into the giant mother-ship, they wafted Thane between them to a chamber filled with gleaming medical instruments.

Thane was guided into a cushioned chair. A soft emerald ray bathed his mind with a low whine.

"Thane Smith," barked Thalkon, standing before him. "You see me. Who am I?"

"I see no one," denied Thane, blank-eyed.

Thalkon sighed. "Turn off the Z-ray. It failed. The psycho-hypnotic field set up by the Morlians can not be penetrated that easily. We must use a drastic remedy. Wheel up the time-warper."

The doctor gasped. "But it's dangerous, Thalkon. One slip and he's lost forever in a mono-chronologic state."

"We'll have to chance it," snapped Thalkon. "It is not violating Galactic Law and using force. We are attempting to save the earthman's mind from a hypnotic block for life."

CHAPTER 11

"Turn the dial back 24 earth-hours. We'll regress Thane Smith in time, back to what his mind was thinking yesterday. Perhaps we can trace what happened to him and Miribel."

A crystal ball above the machine radiated Thane's disjointed, broken thoughts. They were a replay of his life during the past 24 hours. In time, the important part came.

"It's working," exulted Thalkon. "His whole brain has been thrown back in time to *before* he was hypnotized. Now if we can only learn what happened then…."

Thane's thoughts suddenly became the equivalent of a shout.

THE DRIVER… A MORLIAN!… POINTING A TUBULAR WEAPON… SLEEP GAS… OHHHHHH!

His thoughts faded out to nothingness for a while, but then they gradually came back, faintly at first, then more clearly.

Sailing above Pacific Ocean… SAUCER DIVING… WE'LL CRASH… No, we slid underwater smoothly…amazing…going down, down…

Thalkon leaned forward tensely, listening to the telepathic spray of thought.

Down to sea bottom itself…small glow, growing bigger… A GIANT DOME!

Thalkon snapped off the time-warper. "That's all we need to know. The sea bottom, eh? One of their secret bases."

"But now," said the doctor, "can we bring Smith's mind back to the present? Or will his thoughts circle endlessly through that experience hours ago?"

Slowly, carefully, the doctor turned a dial. The purling violet beam slowly shaded into deep purple, indigo, azure, cerulean blue. The machine's whine rose to an inaudible pitch.

"More power," yelled Thalkon.

"If the time-warper overloads, it will explode."

But the doctor turned it up another notch. A swirling amethyst color now suffused the beam aimed at Thane's head. Suddenly, a needle calibrated in hours, minutes and seconds swung over.

The doctor shut off the time-warper, wiping his brow. "He's back. All is well. But it was close…close."

Thane's eyes lost their blankness. "Thalkon! But how did I get here? Last I remember, I was down in the sea dome with a ray pointing at me…"

"A double success," said Thalkon to the doctor. "The time regressions not only bypassed the hypnotic spell, but when his mind returned to the present, the psycho-hypnotic field was broken completely. He's de-hypnotized."

Briefly, Thalkon described to Thane on the most recent events and handed over the manuscript Thane had written the night before.

"Drivel," said Thane.

"The Morlians hypnotized you to utterly disbelieve in saucers, hoping to use you to cover their tracks completely. We had to break down your hypno-spell somehow, in order to find out where Miribel is."

"She's still their prisoner," exclaimed Thane, leaping up.

"But you can guide a rescue party to the sea dome," said Thalkon. "Miribel is one of our best planetary agents, male or female. If the Morlians succeed in breaking clown her psycho-shield, they'll learn many of our secrets. I'll make arrangements for the rescue party."

* * * *

Thane looked over the rescue party, shocked.

"Meet TeeZee," said Thalkon, waving at a small humanoid 3½ feet tall. "That's a short version of his unpronounceable name, Tz-kkjqqg."

The little humanoid had an oversized head, large wrap-around eyes, hardly any nose at all, a slit-like mouth, and a pointed chin. A description of the little men stepping from landed saucers, given over and over again in Sheel's book, Thane remembered.

"And this is HiBaLuKy," introduced Thalkon, and Thane gaped again at a creature 8 feet tall, with gangly arms and legs, a round pumpkin head, in which there was set only one eye—in front.

"He has an eye in the back too," said Thalkon. "Special evolutionary pattern in his world. And I'm the last member of our team." Thalkon went on smilingly. "The Galactic Vigilantes are recruited from 768,981 worlds. Only the best men—or creatures, if you prefer—are chosen for duty. They may look like grotesque 'freaks' to you, Thane, but have no illusions as to their intelligence or abilities. No earthman is their equal."

* * * *

Their gleaming silver saucer tilted and dove into the ocean. "If you've guessed anywhere within a hundred miles of the true position, we'll find the dome," said Thalkon.

It shone way off to the left, finally.

Thane had a sudden belated question. "But how are four…uh… men going to invade a dome swarming with Morlians, and snatch a prisoner away from them? The moment they see us…"

"They won't," said Thalkon, turning to move a lever. "We will of course use our anti-visio field." Thane noticed that everything in the ship became a bit hazy.

"You mean invisibility?" he gasped. But that was not so odd. In certain eerie sightings, in Sheel's book, UFO's had been detected by radar, but were never seen. Other UFOs were also unseen though their whine could be distinctly heard, while still others would abruptly 'wink out' in midair.

Silent and unseen, their saucer 'oozed' through the dome's shell. A Morlian guard on duty did not turn his head.

"You don't know just where Miribel was imprisoned?" whispered Thalkon.

Thane shook his head.

"No matter," said Thalkon. "TeeZee, do your part."

The dwarf humanoid's large owl eyes began to glow, brighter and brighter.

"X-rays?" guessed Thane.

"No, it is what you earth-people call clairvoyance—seeing at a distance. It's a psychic sense these humanoids have always possessed, besides normal vision. He'll refocus everywhere in the dome, through solid walls, until he spies Miribel…"

"I see her," said the little man, in a low rumble deeper than any human voice.

TeeZee gave some kind of mathematical phrases that seemed to tell Thalkon exactly where to guide their saucer, in the big open part of the dome. Their craft then slanted down toward a chamber on the flooring.

Thane tensed. Through a ceiling window, he could see Miribel strapped in a seat, with Morlians shining rays at her head from all sides. He could faintly detect the strain on her face; obviously, she was battling with all her mental powers to keep her psychic shield from breaking down.

"Hurry," snapped Thane. "That girl is undergoing torture."

Thalkon was reading an instrument. "Hmm, walls made of plasto-X which would resist our blast-rays for long minutes. That would raise the alarm. HiBaLuKy, your turn."

Swiftly, the giant alien held up one arm and pointed with a long rubbery finger. His body began to glow strangely with a crackling noise.

"His people," informed Thalkon, "are living dynamos. Electrical generators. He's building up a high voltage." Thalkon pressed a button and a porthole slid open, where the giant's finger pointed.

His arm began to crackle, then his hand. Suddenly, from his finger, hissed a long lightning-like streak, one that did not wink out but remained. It touched the wall of the chamber and began making a circle.

Like an oxy-acetylene torch slicing through steel, the electrical flame ate its way through the plasto-X barrier. The 6-foot-wide plate abruptly fell outward.

"Let's go," snapped Thalkon. The three of them catapulted out of the porthole, dove through the air without falling, and streaked into the breach.

"Hey, you left me behind," shouted Thane angrily. He saw that the Morlians were taken by surprise, as the Vigilantes used small hand-weapons to paralyze them Miribel was ripped loose from her seat and wafted to the hole in the wall.

Then Thane saw them coming, a dozen Morlians sailing through the air grimly, weapons in hand. The alarm had sounded. His friends would not have time to emerge from the prison chamber, Thane saw with a sinking heart.

CHAPTER 12

But the Morlians had opened fire now, as Thalkon's party swam out of the hole. Holding his breath, Thane punched buttons, those controlling level flight at low speed—he hoped.

Smoothly, the saucer slid forward. It was still invisible so the Morlians were not alarmed. Thane punched again, tilting at a slight angle down. Another button and he was pointed straight at the floating Morlians.

Now! He jabbed the 'spurt speed' button. The saucer sprang forward like a battering ram. Invisible it might be but it was still solid in texture. With grim satisfaction, Thane saw a dozen Morlian bodies flung helter-skelter, probably with broken bones if not worse.

"Good work, Thane," came a beamed telepathic cry from Thalkon as he led their party into the porthole. Miribel had fainted.

Thalkon leaped to the controls. "We must leave fast before they get their craft after us, here in the dome."

But even as their saucer spun upward, an ash-silver, domed disk came whistling toward them. A livid green ray swept widely in a circle and finally touched their saucer. There was a jolt and sparks.

"Burned out our anti-visio unit," panted Thalkon. "Now they can let loose at us with blaster-rays." He turned, yelling "Stop!"

But it was too late. TeeZee and HiBaLuKy were floating out the hatchway, lugging a big blaster with them. Thane saw how they planted themselves squarely in front of the Morlian ship, raking it from stem to stern—if it had a stem or stern.

It was a delaying tactic. It forced the ship to turn and first eliminate the daring pair with their big blaster-ray. Thane shuddered, and Thalkon put his hand to his eyes, as a scarlet beam from the Morlians touched the tiny man and the giant, turning them into two burning torches.

"They gave their lives to save us," half-sobbed Thalkon. He was already punching buttons. Their saucer now had a clear path up to the dome's roof, where it oozed through swiftly. Morlian pursuit craft appeared behind them, but Thalkon grinned.

"Since when do they think they can ever catch a Vigilante ship?"

Their saucer ripped up through the ocean at fantastic speed, creating a tremendous wake. The Morlian ships faded in the murk, hopelessly outclassed.

Miribel came to just as the saucer shot up into the air, shedding a shower of water drops.

"The sun," breathed Miribel thankfully. "I never thought I'd see it again." Her indigo eyes turned.

"I'm glad to see you too, Thane Smith."

Thane was glad too, at the way her hand clung to his.

* * * *

Thalkon now stood before what looked like a microphone with a stern face, but no words came from his lips.

"Beamed telepathy," said Miribel, "to our mother-ship. I'll translate his message—*Attention, headquarters. Another Morlian base discovered at sea bottom in Pacific Ocean. Send blaster-fleet. Exact position as follows…*."

Miribel then waved and telepathically triggered their wall monitor screen to show what followed. Thane saw the mother-ship hanging 1000 miles high. From it spewed forth saucers with turrets and wicked-looking dish aerials which were impulse-projectors, not receivers. A hundred of them dived down through the atmosphere and plunged into the Pacific Ocean.

Thane watched in awe as the 'blaster-fleet' reached the sea dome and let loose with a barrage of rays. A dozen Morlian craft emerged to give battle but were quickly blasted into a shower of sparks—like the dogfight Thane had seen.

Then the giant dome itself dissolved in one mighty geyser of sparks, completely disintegrated.

Thane was shaken, and disturbed. "If you Galactic Vigilantes are pledged to aid worlds without using methods of force and with respect for lives, how do you explain this? At least a thousand Morlians died before our eyes."

Miribel stared at him, surprised. "Thane, didn't you know? We have never killed a Morlian yet."

Thane, in turn, stared at her in surprise. "After what I saw? And don't forget during that dogfight I watched, the Morlian ship was blown to bits, including its Morlian crew."

"But it is only their *ship* that disintegrates," said Miribel. "Not the pilots. You see, ahead of each blast beam goes the Nth-beam. This instantaneously teleports any *living* thing aboard into the Nth dimension we told you about, just before the ship explodes. And there we have a gigantic prison, so to speak, where all teleported Morlians are put into custody for rehabilitation."

"Do the Morlians retaliate in kind, if they happen to blast a Vigilante ship?"

Miribel shook her head, sadly. "You saw what happened to TeeZee and HiBaLuKy down in the sea dome when we escaped. They were consumed by nuclear fire. Morally, despite their high technological state, the Morlians are ruthless savages."

Thalkon now turned to them in satisfaction. "One more Morlian base wiped out. But there are others we have not yet found. If only we had a spy…."

He was staring at Thane. "…we have one, named Thane Smith."

Thane was too taken aback to say anything, waiting for Thalkon to explain himself.

"Ponder this. The Morlians do not know that we seized you, after your brainwashing, and de-hypnotized you. Nor did they see you in our scout ship that rescued Miribel. You never came out of the ship."

Thane nodded, getting the idea. "In other words, as far as the Morlians know, I'm still their brainwashed dupe."

"And as such," added Thalkon, "you can pretend to still be hypnotized and on their side, so to speak."

"Now wait a minute," objected Thane. "If they can read my mind, they would instantly know my thoughts and realize I was back to normal. They would also know I was working with you."

"Not if we brainwash you in a different way, earth-man. We can mold your mental faculties to form an invisible psycho-shield around your mind. Then you will have the power to conceal your true thoughts and only release those you want."

"You mean I'll be able to turn my thoughts 'on and off' at will?"

"Just as we do," said Thalkon. "Now, are you willing to be our spy and uncover Morlian secrets? We will give you a tiny device that will secretly pick up and record *their* thought-waves. Through that, we may be able to learn vital enemy secrets or plans. Any little thing will aid us. Well, Thane Smith?"

* * * *

It was in a comfortable room of the mother-ship, in orbit around earth, that Thalkon and Miribel started to brief Thane.

"The earliest life in the galaxy arose some 10 billion years ago. More billions of years passed before civilizations on scattered planets achieved various ways of intergalactic travel. For a long stretch of time, there was only occasional contact between worlds, a slow uprise of galactic trade, and of course wars. Wars sometimes in which a hundred worlds on each side would be pitted against each other. But in time, a new concept arose—cooperation for the betterment of all worlds. And so was formed the United Worlds of the Milky Way Galaxy, a billion-odd years ago. Present member-ship of the UW is almost three million planets. Total population on all those three million planets," went on Thalkon inexorably, "is 6 quadrillions, or 6 million billions. About half are true humans, the rest a wide variety of humanoids and non-humanoids. The latter you might call monster-men."

He paused, then resumed.

"In its councils," he said, "the UW soon authorized the Galactic Vigilantes, a patrol force to roam the galaxy and institute basic law and order, with recruits from any world, human or otherwise."

"Then you've been policing the universe for almost a billion years." Thane was dazed, trying to grapple with these gargantuan figures. "You began at the time when life had barely started on earth."

Thalkon nodded. "We first visited earth about 750 million years ago, on a routine flyby, noting it was in an early stage of evolution and would not produce thinking beings for a long time to come."

Miribel spoke up. "Of course, Thalkon, by saying 'we' you do not mean you and me, but the Vigilantes of that ancient time." She turned. "Naturally, Thane, membership changes as time goes on and Vigilantes die to be replaced by others. Worlds have also died of what you might call old age, during that time, while new worlds freshly reaching a peak of civilization took their place. Our world Zyl joined the UW only a million years ago. We are a comparatively young planet."

"If you can stand more," said Thalkon sympathetically, "the Vigilantes today number some 25 million members and 10 million spacecraft."

Thane whistled. "But then, they have some 3 million worlds to patrol."

"And protect," reminded Thalkon, "like earth. The youngest planets, either isolated or just emerging into the stage of space travel, must be guarded from rapacious worlds—like Morli. At last count, there were 128,000 maverick or piratical planets in the galaxy, whose aims are often to plunder, conquer, or otherwise plague helpless worlds."

"Over 100,000 lawless worlds," mused Thane. He looked up at Thalkon in sudden realization. "Lord, how many times in the past have the Vigilantes driven predator planets away from earth?"

"On the average, once every 5000 years, or 200 times since early mankind arose on earth about two million years ago."

"Two hundred times! What were they all after?"

"It would take too long to recite," Thalkon said. "I'll give you some highlights. About a million years ago, the Blue Worlds piratical fleet came and attempted to rifle your whole world of all its uranium ore, in order to build up their arsenal of nuclear weapons. Only dim-witted man-apes were around to see...."

"Eventually, our Vigilante forces won out and drove the defeated enemy back into outer space, its power broken for a thousand years. But let me tell you of a raid on earth that succeeded, partly at least."

CHAPTER 13

"An insectal race, busily setting up apparatus and processing the soil, the Midge World escaped our notice for a century," admitted Thalkon ruefully. "During that time, they set up mining camps all over earth and quietly extracted every bit of an element called technetium. Technetium is a metal that acquires negative weight under electrical stimulus. In short, it is an antigravity agent, from which giant floating barges can be made to transport a world's goods with ease."

"And the Midge World thieves got away with it all?"

"Several million tons, even though technetium was the rarest element on earth at the time. Remember, they had a full century to work. The Vigilantes did not catch on until they had finished their planetary larceny. By then it was too late to stop them or take their technetium away. We simply quarantined their world from any further space commerce for the next million years, to teach them a lesson. Take Atlantis, for example. Despite doubts among earth archeologists and authorities, it did exist about 25,000 years ago. But it was a city of heartbreak and tyranny. Millions of humans were subjugated by their space masters, who were humans of a monstrous sort...."

"When one of our cruisers came across this gross slavery of a world—and after all we cannot visit every world too often—the Vigilantes moved in and attempted to smash the power of the slave masters. Facing defeat, they savagely sabotaged the whole island which sank, as in your legends."

"All humans on Atlantis died in that tragic holocaust," put in Miribel softly, "along with their mad masters."

"Mankind fell into decline after that. But emergency squads were sent from the Planetary Reclamation and Rehabilitation Bureau of the Vigilantes to help re-establish civilization in the following centuries."

Thalkon manipulated a movie screen that showed a mighty pyramid being built in ancient Egypt. But there were no long lines of toiling men hauling giant blocks up wooden inclines, as the scene had been reconstructed by archeologists.

Instead, a series of flying saucer disks were coming and going, each with a stone block suspended under it by invisible forces, which was neatly deposited in place.

"Yes," said Thalkon, "we helped build the pyramids which, as you may or may not know, were not just tombs for Pharaohs but…."

"Astronomical stations," interrupted Thane, remembering this from Sheel's UFO book. "The sides by extension gave the size of earth. Certain peephole passages focused on the moon at high and low tides. The passage of the sun, planets, and stars across the sky could be tracked accurately by specific sightings from within the pyramid."

"Let me tell you of one more threat to earth by a self-seeking world." The screen, at Thalkon's wave, now mirrored a huge belted planet with a great reddish spot plus a smaller yellowish blob.

"Jupiter?" guessed Thane.

Suddenly, the yellow spot belched forth from the planet's seething surface and spun away through space.

"The Kull people did that with powerful electro-gravitic forces. A blazing comet was formed, more gigantic than ever known before, which grazed earth and caused chaos. Its name was Venus."

Something clicked in Thane's mind. "Immanuel Velikovsky's theory. Sheel's book went into that briefly. Twice in recorded history—around 2800 B.C. and again in 1200 B.C.—the Venus-comet seared earth, even causing it to flip over and change its axis and rotation."

"The result," Thalkon added, "was worldwide destruction."

Thane grinned wryly. "We're arrogant enough on earth to believe we accomplished everything ourselves, from discovering fire to achieving civilization, without outside aid or protection from vandal planets. We even think that if life exists elsewhere, we are still the highest form of civilization known. In context with what you've told me, that's the greatest joke in the universe."

Miribel smiled at him, pleased. "You are learning fast, Thane. Just as the child must live his own life by trial and error in order to become a full man, so too must each world guide its own destiny and learn by its mistakes."

"That is why, Thane," said Thalkon, very gravely now, "we have not descended upon you in full force, bearing gifts of science and the blueprint for a super-civilization. None of it would do any good, in the long run. Earth must struggle to that goal itself, long and hard though the road may be. Even our presence here, as unseen guardians, must be kept secret because..."

"Because it might throw earth into a turmoil?" ventured Thane.

"That's right," nodded Thalkon.

CHAPTER 14

Thalkon waved, as if dismissing something trivial "Now that you have been allowed to know something, if not everything, about our Vigilante mission, will you agree to be our spy among the Morlians?"

Thane brushed a hand through his hair. "I suppose if I said no, you would hand me some patriotic clichés. It's for the good of my world. How can I let my fellow earthmen down? Can I stand by and see all humanity enslaved? But you know, none of those noble or high-sounding phrases stir me at all. I'm no crusader or knight in armor, shining or otherwise."

Thalkon's face fell and Miribel looked aghast.

Thane went on grimly: "But I'll do it for one reason. I'm still burned up at those three MIB's who tried to rough me up. No Morlian SOB's can pull that on me and get away with it. So I'm your boy."

Thalkon smiled in relief and Miribel took Thane's hand. "You are a brave man," she said.

"Not brave," denied Thane. "If I went back now to my former life, I'd be utterly bored. I've got to do the spy bit just for kicks. Besides, I'm in too deep to back out."

"It will be dangerous, Thane…" Her voice caught a little and she turned away.

Thane's pulse leaped. "I'll be back, Miribel. Maybe I've got a good reason to."

As down in the undersea dome, a wired helmet rested over Thane's head. But this time it was not a Morlian but a Vigilante 'brainwasher'.

"What we will do," explained Thalkon, groping for simple words, "is beam psychons into your brain."

"Psychons?"

"The basic units of thought, just as electrons and protons are units of matter."

"I don't get it," grunted Thane, "but go on."

"The psychons will so energize your brain that it will then have the power to put a psychic shield around your mind, at will. You will be able to hide your true mental processes from the Morlians and fool them into thinking you're still their dupe."

"Okay, shoot," said Thane. "I'll take your word for it." It was a peculiar sensation, somewhat like invisible syrup pouring into his mind, as the helmet glowed in deep violet colors. Thane could almost feel his brain gaining 'muscle'. It was over in a moment.

Thalkon removed the helmet then said, "I am going to try to read your mind now. See if you can stop me." Thane felt a subtle mental force from Thalkon, probing into his brain. How could he make his mind blank, Thane wondered. Should he silently say 'stop' to the probe, or what? But even as these thoughts flashed into his mind, the probe turned aside as if meeting a stone wall.

Thalkon kept it up for a minute longer, then relaxed and smiled at Thane. "Perfect. Your psychic-shield sprang up and held firm, even though I used a 100-psycho-powered brain-wave as a probe. No Morlian can do 90 on that scale. You are safe from their mind-reading abilities."

"But won't that immediately arouse their suspicions?" Thane said. "If they suddenly find themselves unable to read my mind, where they could before, they'll know I've been given a psycho-shield—by you."

"Ah, but you will be able to give them a 'mind' to read. The kind of conscious mind they left you with after they hypno-conditioned you to disbelieve in flying saucers. You will allow those thought-patterns to flow outside the psycho-shield. Reading that false 'mind,' they will be satisfied you are still the same."

"I get it," nodded Thane. "I just keep thinking 'aloud,' so to speak, that UFO s don't exist while secretly, behind my psycho-shield, I'm thinking what SOB's the MIB's are. Great."

"You perceive things quickly," said Thalkon approvingly.

Miribel came in, wanting to know how it had gone with Thane.

"Fine," he answered her aloud. "Try reading my mind."

Miribel probed for a moment then smiled. "Blank. You have put up a psycho-shield."

"Yes," continued Thane's thoughts, hidden by the shield. "And now I can boldly state that you are more lovely than any earth girl I've ever known and…."

He broke off, startled at his own thoughts. Then, to Thalkon: "Well, now I'm ready to tackle the Morlians. What are my instructions?"

"To go back to your cabin and continue your campaign against UFO sightings, as the Morlians conditioned you to do before we de-hypnotized you. Use any and all methods you can think of to heap scorn on saucer sightings. That way, you will gain the confidence—and gratitude—of the Morlians. Sooner or later, they may reveal key things about themselves. But not consciously, of course."

Thalkon snapped his fingers and a drawer in the wall opened. A small device levitated itself into his hand. It was a thin wafer with tiny symmetrical dots on it.

"This psycho-detector will pick up hidden thoughts of the Morlians, when they get careless, and beam them to our receiving unit."

"Where will I carry it?" Thane wanted to know.

"Next to your brain, under your skull."

Thane jerked. "You mean…uh…surgery?"

Thalkon laughed. "Why use such a primitive technique? Remember how our craft 'oozed' through the sea dome's wall?" He had fixed the metal wafer into a gun-like device, pressing the muzzle against Thane's forehead. A burst of radiation and Thalkon said quietly, "It's done. The wafer's vibrational rate was changed so that it penetrated through the skin and bone and implanted itself next to your brain."

* * * *

Thane watched the silvery saucer vanish in the sky, then looked around his cabin. Nothing had changed since he had last left. He pondered a moment, then made a phone call. After hanging up, he sat at his typewriter and its rattle went out of the window into the growing darkness.

Thane heard a purring sound and turned. A big black car drove up. The three MIB's—the same three as before—knocked on the door. Thane drew in a deep breath, giving himself a command. He could almost feel the psycho-shield closing in around his mind.

"Hello?" said Thane as if puzzled, as he opened the door.

"Thane Smith?"

"Yes. But who are you...?"

"You haven't seen us before?" came the query.

"Of course not. Is this some joke?"

The three Morlians glanced at one another, pleased. Another question came. "Do you believe in flying saucers, Thane Smith?"

"Listen, if you're three nut UFOlogists, trying to convince me UFO's from other worlds exist, you're wasting your time." He turned and grabbed up typewritten pages. "As a matter of fact, I've just written up a radio broadcast I'm making tonight over station KZQQ in Grover City. My old pal, John Winkle, gave me room on his *I Wonder* program. My speech will roast all saucer believers until they're not rare, not medium, but well-done."

Thane tossed down the papers in disgust. "Believe me, gentlemen, I'm sick and tired of hearing about kooks, crackpots, and screwballs claiming they see mysterious objects in the sky. So don't try to sell me on saucers."

The three men arose to go. "Too bad you won't listen to our proof that flying saucers exist," said one with a faint smile of irony, the best his wooden face could do.

For the first time, the Morlians let their guard down and a silent thought was picked up by Thane's psycho-detector wafer, beaming it to outer space. Thane found, to his surprise, that the wafer's contact also allowed him to 'hear' the Morlian as he thought, 'Our brainwashing worked better than we expected. The earthman actually thinks we are saucer believers! Everyone will have a laugh when we return to the Antarctic base.'

Thane stiffened. *Antarctic base!* One of the unknown Morlian strongholds had already been exposed, inadvertently. Thalkon, at the psycho-receiver, must be rubbing his hands in joy.

The Morlians left, satisfied that Thane was their brainwashed dupe. The joke of it all was that they did not even know Thane was no longer concerned with merely exposing them, or his Vigilante friends, to the world. And what a shock it would be to the Morlians if they knew he was now a Vigilante spy.

The picture had changed for Thane. He was playing for bigger stakes now. Simply revealing to the world that UFO's did exist and were manned by extraterrestrial people would not in the least defeat the Morlian plot, whatever it was. In fact, exposure of the Vigilantes might hamper their efforts to counteract the Morlian threat.

Thane suddenly realized, with a little whistle, that he was now as anxious to avoid giving proof of UFO's as the Morlians. So he sat eagerly at his typewriter again, to finish his forthcoming radio speech discounting all saucer sightings. He was not only 'fooling' the Morlians into thinking he was 'following instructions' but also wholeheartedly keeping up the smokescreen hiding UFO's from earth-people.

Thane grinned wryly. A strange, ironic situation. He began banging the keys.

* * * *

"Greetings, Thane Smith!" a voice boomed in his mind an hour later and Thane's fingers mashed down on the keys, locking a half-dozen. As he unhooked them, sheepishly, the silent telepathic voice went on:

"This is Thalkon psycho-transmitting. You see, the wafer near your brain is a two-way contact. Good work, Thane! We picked up the relayed thought of the Morlian about an Antarctic base."

"I guess my spy stint paid off pretty quickly at that," radiated back Thane, knowing his beamed thought-message would reach Thalkon.

"As a reward," went on Thalkon, "we will let you see the result, in relayed psycho-vision scenes from Antarctica. They will be live, in full color."

Sounds like a TV ad, thought Thane in amusement. Into his mind suddenly sprang a vivid scene of the Antarctic ice-cap as seen from space. Then, as if he were aboard one of the diving Vigilante ships, the scene enlarged in detail and narrowed its scope to one portion of the mighty ice-sheet somewhere in the area known as Little America.

"As soon as we got the tip," came in Thalkons psycho-voice, like a commentator, "we rushed scout ships to Antarctica. Using the anti-visio screen, they snooped around while their detecto-beams revealed exactly where the Morlian base was. Now watch, as our demolition fleet does its job."

The panorama in Thane's mind, like a motion-picture screen, now showed the fleet of turreted saucers which had turned visible and were diving down at blistering speed. Livid red rays sprang from them, melting the ice in a wide circle. Into the newly created 'lake' plunged the fleet, melting ice ahead as fast as they flew down.

"We could not use the Morlian ice-tunnels," interposed Thalkon, "which led a mile down to the bottom of the ice-cap, without being detected and opposed. Sudden attack was our best bet. Hence, the use of infrabeams to melt the ice for a direct attack."

And now, as the last ice barrier melted, it splashed down into what had formerly been a huge hollow, holding the Morlian base. Before any alarm system could work, the Vigilante blast-beams were at work, wiping out the base methodically.

It was, thought Thane to himself, like a child erasing a picture on a blackboard.

Thane felt his blood turn cold at the ruthless wiping out of Morlian lives, whether they deserved it or not…then he abruptly remembered and relaxed. The Vigilantes never killed. Morlians were being hurled alive and well, an instant before the blast-ray stuck, into the Nth dimension, there to be imprisoned.

In moments it was done. Shattered wreckage lay underneath the Antarctic ice-cap a mile deep, where the Morlians had hidden their secret base from earthly eyes. The water flooding down from the hole melted by the Vigilante fleet was already filling the artificial hollow and freezing. The fleet turned upward, splashing up through the mile-deep lake they had created. In free air, they sped off into space.

CHAPTER 15

"Look," exclaimed Thane, as the last scene of Antarctica faded out. "A party of explorers, probably from the South Polar camp, happened to come by and saw the fleet shooting away. Those are mostly scientists. Thalkon. What if they report their unmistakable sighting, plus the incredible 'lake' melted in the ice?"

"Come, Thane," returned Thalkon unperturbed. "It is not that easy to convince your unenlightened world that saucers from outer space are here. Even scientists are discredited when they claim to report sightings."

Right, thought Thane to himself. Sheel's book had made that plain. Scientists, as a group, were perhaps the greatest saucer-phobes of all, arrogantly believing no spacecraft could ever cross the vastness of space simply because earth technology had no such vehicles, nor any remotely reasonable plan to devise them.

"Our greatest protection against exposure," broke in Thalkon, as if following Thane's ruminations, "has always been humanity's overwhelming egocentrism. The belief or feeling that they are 'special' creatures, unmatched in the universe. The unwillingness of the human mind to entertain the thought that beings with an intelligence a magnitude above them can possibly exist, or visit earth. It has made our job easier.

"Another Morlian base crossed off the list," said Thalkon in momentary triumph. Then his psycho-voice fell. "But how many more to go? And when will we ever locate their main base? Until we destroy that, our mission is unfinished and earth remains in danger."

In danger of *what?* Thane wanted to know desperately but knew Thalkon would only answer, "It is not permitted to tell." If it wasn't simply conquest of earth or enslavement of the human race, as Thalkon had said before, then what was it? What could be still worse, as Thalkon had implied. Would Thane ever find out?

"It is not likely," Thalkon's voice came back, and Thane jumped. Damn, he had forgotten to put up his psycho-shield. "It is for your own good that you do not know." Thalkon went on soothingly. "There are some things the human mind is not geared to absorb or withstand. It is something that can only be described with your words—'ghastly' or 'fiendish.' More I will not say."

Thane shuddered a little, then shrugged. "Okay, Thalkon. But it's time now for me to rush to my radio broadcast in Grover City. About an hour's drive. Bye now."

* * * *

At the KZQQ mikes, Thane put on what he thought was a terrific performance as a UFO antagonist. It might put him in the class of Dr. Dennis T. Wengler, the 'arch enemy' of flying saucers according to UFOlogists, who airily attributed all saucer phenomena to mirages, atmospheric tricks, and optical illusions. Or at the least, Thane would be alongside Perry Klausner, the electrical engineer who proclaimed that his 'plasmoids'—natural conglomerates of ionized plasma—could account for most UFO's.

Thane's broadcast came up with a third major concept denigrating UFO's as illusions. He keyed his opening line in neatly with the program he was on—*I Wonder*.

"Do you wonder if UFO's are machines—or myths?" began Thane. "Or if flying saucers are real—or just flying specks in the eye? Are they Unidentified Flying Objects—or Unequivocal Fooler Orbs? Do you wonder, as I did?"

He took a breath, then thundered, "My friends, I am here to tell you that you have more chance of seeing genuine *sorcerers* than saucers."

To the side, John Winkle was beaming. This fiery oration on the nation's most controversial subject should jack up the rating of his *I Wonder* program nicely. Phone calls, telegrams, letters would pour in.

Thane went on. "I'm not just talking through my hat. I've discovered exactly what the so-called saucers and UFO's are. You've all seen the strange shapes clouds can make? Well, unknown to science or the astronauts yet, there are clouds in *space*."

Thane paused dramatically. "Those space clouds, made up of random dust that gravitated together, are too small and tenuous to be seen in telescopes or detected by space probes. Only my special *orthoconic oscillometer* was able to spot them."

Thane rolled his eyes upward—luckily it wasn't television—at this magnificent lie.

"The small space clouds exist in huge swarms, all around earth. And they cast *shadows*, you see. Now it is a peculiar aspect of these space clouds that, through gravitic and electromagnetic forces from the sun, they assume rather geometrical shapes—disks, cigars, ovals, globes, even pyramids and rhomboids."

Thane swallowed down an intense desire to chuckle and went on in mock-earnest tones. "You recognize those shapes, eh? Of course you do. They are what sighters so often breathlessly report—disks, cigars, ovoids, globes, pyramids, rhomboids, and the rest. They all *seem* to be too regular in form to be natural but—"

Thane choked down another hysterical impulse to guffaw and finished, "But that is all that the kooks and crackpots see—*cloud shadows* from outer space!"

Thane expanded on this theme in more detail for the rest of his half-hour. He had taken care, at home, to make his theory superficially consistent and plausible—in a sort of crazily implausible way.

"Yes, a cloud in space far away would throw a huge shadow on earth. But remember that these are small clouds, and it is only their tiny dense *cores* that can throw shadows. Furthermore, it is only the shadow's umbra—the sharp central portion—which is projected down into earth's atmosphere. Hence, when spied by gullible witnesses, they report UFO's anywhere from 25 feet to 500 feet wide or more."

Thane drove on, determined to please the Morlians who were undoubtedly listening in. "And notice how scientifically valid my discovery is. The clouds, being light, are subject to every 'breeze' of the solar-wind in space—the streams of electrons and protons the sun constantly emits throughout interplanetary space. Even if the solar-breeze only moves the cloud an inch, this movement would be magnified, through its long-range shadow, into many linear miles. That is why the UFO's seem to dart through the sky at such blinding speeds. Then, when a gust of the variable solar-wind blows the cloud to a stop, the UFO-shadow on earth seems to stop on a dime."

The small studio audience began clapping loudly. Thane knew that if he had won them, he had also captured most of the millions in the radio audience.

"And think, UFO's almost always move *silently*—as do shadows. They display no rocket discharges or other visible means of propulsion—shadows don't either."

Applause interrupted Thane again. He waited, then resumed.

"As for the color changes reported by so many witnesses, these space clouds contain in them tiny bits of grit with jagged edges. Like ice-crystals that create our rainbows, these gritty particles act like a filter and split sunlight up into its separate rays at times—red, orange, green, blue, yellow. In other words, they throw rainbow-hued shadows that can change color with quixotic rapidity—as in the majority of UFO sightings."

Clapping came again, loudest this time from one corner. Glancing there, Thane started. Three intense pairs of eyes stared back at him. The MIB's! They were obviously highly pleased with their 'dupe's' anti-UFO tirade.

Luckily, Thane had put up his psycho-shield the moment he had arrived, just in case. He did not know whether the Morlians always posed as 'men-in-black' or adopted other guises when infiltrating among humans.

Thane ended his broadcast with the aplomb of other pompous egotists who believed they had single-handedly solved the UFO riddle: "So there is little question that UFO's are merely the shadows of the space clouds, thrown into earth's atmosphere. Next time any kook tells you he saw a 'craft' land and little green, purple, or orange men step out, you'll know that he embellished his story after seeing a shadow-saucer. I'm sure scientists and authorities will immediately see how my revelation has once and for all solved the UFO phenomenon. Good night."

At the door, Thane was not surprised to find the three MIB's approaching him. "We wish to congratulate you. Thane Smith," said one, extending his hand. "We belong to a group that is fighting this ridiculous belief in flying saucers from other worlds."

Thane could hardly force down the grin that threatened to crease his lips. In posing as earthmen, the Morlians were trying to fool the one person on earth they couldn't fool. The one who alone knew all about them.

Thane let go of the rather clammy hand, carefully keeping his psycho-shield up. "Then we're on the same side, gentlemen," he said, "aren't we?"

That was Thane's mission, to gain their confidence. "We are," nodded one MIB solemnly. "In fact, we have an idea how you can further explode the saucer myth. May we come and see you at your place tomorrow?"

Thane pretended to hesitate, not wanting to seem too eager, but then smiled. "I'm rather busy but…well, this matter takes priority. Make it any time you wish. Here's my address."

Thane handed over one of his business cards, on the back of which were printed directions for finding his isolated cabin.

"Thank you. We'll see you tomorrow." The MIB's turned away.

Thane was taken aback at the figure that next approached him, in his natty uniform.

"Colonel Taggert!"

"I was in the studio audience," nodded the Air Force officer. He stared curiously at Thane. "Last week you came to me with a saucer sighting and photographs to back it up. You seemed to be an ardent and convinced believer in UFO's. Now, tonight, you damn them all as chimeras. Why the abrupt change of heart, Smith?"

Amusement rose within Thane. "Why, Colonel," he said blandly, "you yourself told me I had merely seen two hawks fighting it out. That made me see the error of my ways when I thought it over later."

Taggert was shaking his head, shrewdly. "But your photos did not show two hawks…"

"They didn't, Colonel?" said Thane sharply. "Then what did they show?"

"Why…uh…" Taggert was trapped, but obviously thinking fast. "They seemed to show two shiny craft. But then, peculiar reflections could cause this optical illusion—for instance, the shadows of your space clouds?"

Thane bit his lip. *Touché*. But lurking behind all this was something else. The mere fact that Thane's 'change of heart' was questioned meant that Taggert was not so much a pooh-pooher of UFO's as he pretended. Could it also mean that the Air Force secretly *believed* in saucers?

"Yes, my space cloud shadows could account for my photos," agreed Thane. He had to play his new role consistently, before everyone. "Don't you agree that that could explain all UFO sightings?"

Thane was curious to see his reaction. Taggert seemed to be nagged by something, judging by his uncertain smile. Then he went on smoothly, "You know, Thane, *if* there were real UFO's and UFO-beings, who wished to keep their presence on earth a secret, one might almost think they had *bought you off*."

The Colonel chuckled loudly as if to show he was only being facetious. But his eyes narrowly kept on Thane's face.

"My dear Colonel," Thane said, "if you know UFO's to be pure illusion, how can you even talk of their presumed occupants?"

CHAPTER 16

Thane opened the door the next day to let the three MIB's in. They murmured polite greetings and Thane waved them to sit down.

"Now, your big idea, gentlemen?"

"To write a book, Thane Smith."

"Another one debunking UFO's, you mean? But that's been done by Wengler Klausner, and others too."

"No, we mean another kind of book debunking, so to speak, the biggest names in UFOlogy."

They were waiting for his answer. "A great idea," said Thane, without enthusiasm. "I wish I had thought of it myself."

The three MIB's relaxed, and once again Thane stiffened as their hidden thoughts came forth. They were letting their guard down, as the previous three Morlians had, confident that brainwashed Thane was no menace and could in fact help them greatly in their campaign to keep earth ignorant of their presence.

"Latch on, Thalkon," beamed Thane through the psycho-transmitter touching his brain. "Here comes some more spillover from these Morlian thugs."

But the telepathic leaks from their brains were nothing significant. "The earthling is our dupe…."

"He will do anything we say…."

"He may once and for all kill the flying saucer controversy for us…."

"Ah, I've got it," snapped Thane, pacing the floor dramatically. "We want to show that the UFO guys are crackpots, don't we? People with wild imaginations, not to be trusted. Well, in various books, it has been speculated that if the saucers were ships from outer space, they would have *secret bases* from which to operate. Remarks about *secret bases* would make them seem like kooks."

Thane tensed as involuntary thoughts came from the MIB's: "They of course were guessing... They didn't know of our real bases.... The subsea and Antarctic bases that were recently destroyed.... Nor of our bases in the Himalayas, miles underground in Mammoth Cave, out in the Gobi Desert, deep within the Amazon Jungle..."

Thane's pulse leaped with each named spot. Four more bases for the Vigilantes to wipe out. But Thane had another thought and spoke aloud again.

"You know, it's been suggested that the so-called space visitors might have bases on the moon, or Mars, and elsewhere in the solar system. We can hit them there and ruin their reputations."

Again, the unshielded thought-stream of the MIB's came through: "Yes, they have worried us all along by guessing we had interplanetary bases...in Diogenes Crater on the moon...at the Mare Sytoris on Mars...at the North Pole of Venus..."

Thane exulted inwardly. Seven bases revealed! He waited for more, but the three MIB's had arisen, their private thoughts ending, "Then you will write this book smearing UFOlogists in the eyes of the public? That way, Thane Smith, we can smash the whole rotten egg apart and end the belief in UFO's or ships from outer space."

"Right," nodded Thane, opening the door. "I'll start outlining the book immediately, and gathering research data."

Hardly had the MIB's driven away than Thane felt it safe to let down his mental shield and contact Thalkon.

"The jackpot, Thalkon," crowed Thane.

"Yes, just about, Thane," came Thalkon's beamed psycho-waves. "We surmised from various factors that they had no more than a dozen bases on earth, some of which we destroyed before you came into the picture. Now we'll get most or all."

"How about the interplanetary bases? Would the three named cover them all?"

"Not likely," returned Thalkon. "We suspect Morlian bases on Jupiter or its moons, also at Saturn, and perhaps even among the asteroids. But it almost hopeless to search for them on huge worlds or in vast volumes of space."

His telepathic voice became worried. "And I doubt any of the bases revealed would be their main base. I'm sure they've been drilled over and over never to think of where that is, under any circumstances, for fear of the thought being picked up by us. But let us be thankful for lesser favors. Thane, you have been of immeasurable help in our long struggle against the Morlians. We didn't have the slightest chance of stealing thoughts from them, as you did. Only an 'innocent' earthman, with seemingly no mind-reading powers, could have made them let their guard down and hand us tips."

"But when their next seven bases go up in smoke so suddenly," pondered Thane, "won't they suspect that the leak is through me?"

"They might," agreed Thalkon. "Then again they might not. After all, they are unaware that you have been de-brainwashed and that you wear a psycho-unit next to your brain, so why should they even suspect you picked up the information that betrayed seven of their bases? They will attribute it to some new penetrating spy-beam we developed and will hastily outfit their remaining bases with countermeasures."

Thalkon went on slowly. "Still, I cannot order you to remain on the job, seeking the greatest tip-off of all—the location of their main base. If you wish, Thane, we'll pick you up now and whisk you safely into space…"

"It's not often that a man gets a chance to be a hero and save the world," murmured Thane, half-humorously. "Why should I toss it aside? I'll carry on the psycho-battle of wits with the Morlians and see if I can make it a bases-loaded…there's some kind of a pun there…home run."

"Thanks, Thane Smith," said Thalkon simply, but eloquently. "You will see the six bases wiped out at zerotime. We will coordinate a simultaneous attack on them all as soon as possible, perhaps tomorrow."

* * * *

The next day, seven fleets of Vigilante ships pounded home at the same time—four on earth, three in space.

In the snow-capped Himalayas, a base that perched high on an icy crag went up in sheets of flame that rose ten miles into the sky.

Deep within Mammoth Cave, where humans had never stumbled on the lower caverns, the Vigilante ships vibrated into wraiths and oozed down through solid rock to create underground chaos where a Morlian camp had existed before.

In the Gobi Desert, with all preliminary searching for the exact location already done, another contingent of Vigilante warcraft blasted a crater a mile deep, and ten thousand more Morlians were whisked to the Nth dimension as prisoners.

The Amazon Jungle proved a bit tricky, in that a wandering tribe of Indians had unwittingly camped close to the Morlian base, too close for Vigilante radiation-guns to blast loose. Instead, risking detection during the process, the Vigilante squadron used the high-vibrationary technique of gliding through the solid ground and joining up directly under the fort. The blasting forces then let loose annihilated matter and formed a giant pit down which the structures tumbled like broken toys. The Indians were only aware of a deep rumble and mild earthquake tremors.

Out in space even more spectacular attacks were taking place at the same time. Thane's psycho-eye was barely able to take it all in.

At the moon, Diogenes Crater flashed out into brilliant light that no doubt startled a dozen astronomers. They would never guess that 250,000 miles away, space warships had converted a million tons of equipment into atomic ashes.

The face of Mars where its Morlian base was located was turned away from earth, so no telescopes spied the mushrooming cloud of radiance that signaled the abrupt disintegration of an alien camp.

The Vigilante blast squadron did its job at the North Pole with a fantastic pyrotechnic display....

"It is done," sighed Thalkon's psycho-voice, half in triumph, half in relief. "Seven more Morlian bases crossed off our charts."

"One more big one to go," said Thane grimly. "When my three MIB pals drop in next, to see how the book is going, I'll try picking their brains for where their main base is."

* * * *

Three days later, when they did drop in, Thane felt the air of gloom around them. He hardly had to pick up their leak-thought: Seven bases destroyed! How did it happen?

Thane rubbed his hands briskly, nodding at typewritten pages on his desk. "The book's going great, gentlemen. I'm giving Keyhoe a real roasting for mentioning interplanetary bases such as the Diogenes camp on the moon...."

Thane knew he had made a ghastly mistake.

"*Diogenes* camp?" shouted one MIB, leaping to his feet "How did you know *which* crater on the moon to name, out of the thousands that exist there?"

"How did you, Thane Smith?" demanded the second MIB, "unless you somehow read our minds last time, and transmitted the information to the Vigilantes?"

"He must die," said the third MIB, in a gruesomely mild voice, almost as if offering Thane a gift.

Desperately, Thane send a psycho-probe into their minds. But they had their psycho-shields up firmly. Thane could not hope to read their minds and outwit them in the fatal moments to come.

One MIB had hauled a tubular device from his pocket, was starting to aim it Thane, with muscles all tensed and ready, burst into action. He darted his hands down, seized this typewriter, and flung it in one smooth flowing motion. It caught the gun-holding MIB squarely in the chest, making him stagger back with a startled grunt and crash into the wall.

The other two MIB's were pulling their alien guns as Thane kept on the move, diving headlong for his loaded shot-gun in the corner. He swung up the muzzle and pulled both triggers. He aimed between the two Morlians because he could not hope to hit one and then the other.

The powerful blast of buckshot whining between the two MIB's utterly startled them. One of them dropped his gun. The other held onto his gun and swung it toward Thane again—only Thane was already there close to him, swinging the shot-gun by the barrel. A solid *thwack* on the MIB's head and he sank without a groan.

The third MIB rushed at Thane with his bare hands. Thane combined a left hook with a Judo spill and a Karate slash at the neck to reduce the third MIB into a quivering mass of moaning flesh sprawled on the floor.

"When you're able to crawl, gents," hissed Thane, "Get your miserable carcasses out of here. Yes, I fingered your bases, and sooner or later you're all going to remove yourselves from my planet, after the Vigilantes launch the final victory battle."

Slowly, the three MIB's got to their feet and lurched out the door. Hoping to catch them off-guard, in their groggy state, Thane snapped: "Where is your main base?"

But the only leak-thought that came back was—Our main base is located nowhere, somewhere, or anywhere.

When Thane tuned in Thalkon, a moment later, the Vigilante said: "Obviously a nonsense rhyme that has been drilled into every Morlian's mind, to make sure he can never reveal the truth. But now that you've been exposed as our spy-agent, Thane, our last hope is gone of ferreting out that secret. Hereafter, you will be a marked man to all Morlians."

CHAPTER 17

Thane looked back at earth as the silvery scout saucer catapulted into space toward the giant Vigilante mother-ship.

"Take a good look at your home world," said Thalkon softly. "We can never take you back—not until and unless the Morlians are completely defeated and all their MIB agents leave. It would be death for you to step back on earth now."

Thane's eyes were a bit haunted, glued on the receding blue-green globe which had given him birth. Two weeks ago he had been Thane Smith, disbeliever in UFO's. Now he was Thane Smith, believer—and exile. An incredible upheaval in his life. Where would it all end? If the Vigilantes failed to uproot the Morlian's main fortress, in the next 30 or 40 years, Thane's whole life would have to be spent in space.

"You are, in effect, a Vigilante," said Thalkon. "An earth-recruit, we might say."

"Though hardly a voluntary one," said Thane dryly. "Fate sort of dragged me in by the heels." He waved a resigned hand. "But I might as well take on Vigilante duties. I have to do something."

"It has already been so arranged," said Thalkon briskly. "You and another Vigilante are to take a special 'spy-craft' and tour through the solar system in the attempt to find their main base."

"Good," agreed Thane, his spirits lifting slightly at the thought of a thrilling ride among the planets. "Who is the other man?"

"It is not a man."

Thane grunted. "All right, I'll wait and see which weirdo monster-man, from among your multi-world recruits, I team up with. I hope it isn't some critter I've seen in nightmares."

After docking within the mother-ship, Thalkon led Thane to a small flying saucer that bristled all over with sensors on booms.

"Looks like a pincushion," commented Thane.

"Those long-range ultra-electronic sensors can detect the slightest nonrandom vibration in the gravo-electro-psycho spectrum pervading the universe."

"Nonrandom means artificial?" guessed Thane.

"Right," nodded Thalkon. "In short, Morlian equipment. You and your partner will cruise out to Jupiter and beyond, probing for any G-E-P leak that might come from their hidden main base."

"You're sure it's out there somewhere?"

"We're not sure," denied Thalkon honestly. "We're just trying every desperate measure we can think of. We now know the Morlians succeeded in establishing certain spire-antennas on earth that...."

Thalkon broke off and Thane said, "It is not permitted to tell, eh?"

"No, but I can tell you this much," said Thalkon apologetically. "You remember when you interviewed the earth-woman, Theda Ranslick, she told you of the small humanoids—our allies—who used a 'sparkling' device. It was to detect any Morlian installation within miles, which they have been secretly planting all around earth for 75 years. It is part of their unspeakable plot against earth."

"But if you detected such installations, why not simply blast them out of existence?" Thane wanted to know.

Thalkon waved his hands helplessly. "How to tell you of the ingenious technology available to the Morlians, as well as us? They first erected each spire-antenna, then made a...a *tape* of it."

"Like a voice on a tape?"

"Yes, only it is not a voice but a *structure* that is taped by them. And it is taped rigidly in the air where the spire stood, after it had been blasted apart."

Thane's head swam a little. "You mean the spire-antenna still exists but invisibly?"

"And permanently," Thalkon almost groaned. "Just as a taped voice is permanent unless it is wiped out, those 'taped' spires also are eternal. And no device for 'wiping them out' is known to our science technology."

He calmed himself. "So there they stand all around earth, invisible and unknown to your people. When they are ready, the

Morlians can beam radiations from anywhere in space, down to the antennas. Then earth will be completely blanketed by a radiative vortex that will accomplish the most…most fiendish feat ever known in galactic history."

"You think," said Thane half-bitterly, "that if you tell me what that fiendish feat is, I'll lose my mind. Yet if you don't tell me, I'll probably lose my mind sooner. The unknown is always worse than the known."

"Not in this case," said Thalkon firmly. "But now you see why it is imperative for us to locate the main Morlian base—and soon. From that base will come the key ray that triggers off all the taped spire-antennas on earth, dooming the human race."

"Yet you're only sending one ship and two Vigilantes to probe the solar system?"

Thalkon stared at him. "Your ship is Number 4,678. Altogether we're sending out 5,000, one every minute."

"Wow!" breathed Thane, stunned.

Thalkon turned. "Here comes your partner."

Thane braced himself. Would it be a Vigilante horror with ten boneless tentacles?…or fourteen stalk eyes?…or one wearing his skeleton on the outside?

Thane gasped as the figure rounded the ship. "Miribel? You?"

* * * *

The 'pincushion,' as Thane dubbed it, spun away from the mother-ship, swinging into a trajectory whose end point was Jupiter.

"Good," said Miribel. You followed the computerized signals perfectly, Thane. Now you simply increase speed 100 times, to shorten the long journey to Jupiter. The velocity dial is clearly marked off in multiples of speed."

"How do you eliminate inertia, gravity-drag, and all the ordinary laws of physics?"

"Do you have about a year to listen while I explain?" she asked half-tauntingly.

"She said to the primitive ape-man," growled back Thane.

"No, Thane," she returned seriously. "We do not look down upon *you*, the individual earthman. It is your society and its state of unenlightenment we deplore. But the human mind itself has the potential to absorb all our science-technology—in a lifetime of study."

"No, thanks," grunted Thane. "I'll stay dumb. But I can figure out elementary things like the trip to Jupiter. Let's see, 500 miles a second to cover about 500 million miles—a million seconds or… ummm"—Thane had always been a rapid calculator—"about ten days."

"We could get there faster," said the girl, "in one day if we wished. But it will take ten days to brief you on using all the sensors aboard. Come, we'll start."

She pointed at a green-glowing phosphor screen that showed squiggly, irregular patterns of brilliant red at times. "Meteoroid sensor, tabulating every grain of matter that passes within a thousand miles to either side. If a nonrandom object—like a Morlian ship—comes within range, the pattern changes to a symmetrical criss-cross and also changes to the color yellow."

On and on it went, each sensor more ingenious and mind-numbing than the last.

Some hours later, after a meal of foods that tasted strange but delicious to Thane, he yawned. "Time for bed I guess…" he began, then suddenly sat up. "Say, we aren't…well, we aren't chaperoned."

Miribel did not avoid his gaze but stared straight back. "No, we aren't. What is the need of it?"

Her kiss was warm, passionate, promising. She drew back a little. "I know something of your immature love codes on earth. They have long been abandoned by Zyl, my world."

"Yes?" breathed Thane, wondering where this would lead. He was unprepared for her next deliberate words.

"We form marriages to have children also. But before that, love is freely given as wished. Sex goes with it, if both partners are willing. Are you willing, Thane?"

Thane was more than willing.

CHAPTER 18

Jupiter filled the entire sky, an immense banded globe 87,000 miles in diameter. Miribel took the controls and plunged their craft down through the thick murky atmosphere.

"Eight thousand miles deep," murmured Thane in awe. "Equal to earth's diameter."

As the saucer leveled over the enormous surface of this giant planet, Thane stared perplexed. "No ice? And what I see now, I don't believe."

A huge finned creature was swimming through the thick air, like a fish through water.

"Jupiter is neither frozen nor lifeless," gasped Thane.

"Of course not," smiled Miribel, as if amused. "The internal heat of the planet has been trapped for ages, under its atmospheric cloak. One of your scientists suspected the truth, that Jupiter is warm and that there is more life here than on earth."

Everywhere that Thane stared, he saw myriads of airborne creatures of all shapes and sizes, preying on each other. He started. "Look. One of the sensor screens shows nonrandom pattern. A Morlian ship…?"

Miribel hastily punched a readout tape, glanced at it, then relaxed. "One of our ships, 500 miles west of us. Many of our sensor craft are scouring Jupiter's surface, which is 1000 times the size of earth's surface."

"Like searching for the proverbial needle in the haystack," said Thane, hopelessly.

Miribel spun the ship up. "It is a better bet to search the moons of Jupiter."

Rising above the atmosphere, they could see several of the moons shining brightly among the stars. Miribel headed for huge Ganymede and began a monotonous, routine circumnavigation in orbital paths with the sensors probing below. Nothing registered on the sensors for long hours.

"This kind of search bores me," said Thane impatiently. "I'd rather take my chances and go back to earth as your spy. I'd have a better chance of finding out where their main base is."

"You would have no chance at all," contradicted the girl. She punched a button and a sibilant voice filled the cabin. "This is a tape we made of a Morlian beamed broadcast, just after those seven bases that you had pinpointed for us were destroyed. I'll switch on the automatic translator, converting it into your language."

The voice changed to English. "...and it has now been determined that the earthman, Thane Smith, must have operated as a Vigilante agent and used psychomethods to extract information from Morlian minds. The result was seven bases destroyed, more than the Vigilantes accomplished by themselves in 50 years. Thane Smith is hereby declared a prime target for capture, by the Supreme High."

"See?" said Miribel, shuddering. "To the Morlians, you are the most wanted man in the universe."

"Wait," said Thane. "Who's the Supreme High?"

"The chief commander of all Morlian forces in the earth Sector."

"Would his headquarters be at the main base?" demanded Thane.

"Yes."

"And notice they said 'captured,' not killed." Thane was now excited. "Don't you see, Miribel? If I'm captured alive—*deliberately*—I would be taken to the main base, the very place we're combing space for. Then, if I could somehow signal Thalkon..."

Miribel's eyes opened wide. "It could be our great breakthrough," she whispered. "It just could be."

"Then what are we waiting for?" snapped Thane, taking over the controls and slewing the ship around. "We're heading back for earth and Thalkon."

* * * *

Thalkon pursed his lips, staring at Thane. "But we don't know for sure that you would be taken directly before the Supreme High at the Morlian main base."

"Why not?" returned Thane. "It seems I represent the greatest and most dangerous spy-agent they ever knew. Wouldn't the top commander of the Morlians want to see me in person—and *sentence* me?"

Miribel winced, but Thalkon nodded. "It makes sense. They might even have some plan to mentally dissect you—I am sorry to be so brutally blunt, Thane—and thus pick up secrets about us Vigilantes. You have been among us and learned much. Every scrap of information about us they gain would be worthwhile to them."

Miribel stepped between them, her eyes terrified. "You must not go, Thane. Mental dissection is…is *horrible*."

"That is true," said Thalkon honestly. "It means slicing your brain apart, bit by bit, extracting every last memory circuit. A psycho-scalpel is used, not a knife. You would live on through it, in torment, and end up drained of all mentality. An idiot."

Thane's face had gone white at the flesh-crawling words. He stood stiff and unmoving for a long moment. Then he grinned wryly. "I'm going to be an idiot now, despite your warning, and take on that challenge."

"No…no," Miribel half-moaned.

Thane took her hand tenderly. "Look, my star love. I'm not as idiotic as I seem. Remember that my thought-processes and actions are far more alien to the Morlians than yours are. Or more primitive, if you wish. They won't even know I'm trying to outfox them, nor will they ever believe I can. The advantage will be on my side."

Thane went on, half-humorously. "It will be like the man who captures an ape and locks him in a cage with a padlock, not knowing that meanwhile, the ape stole the key."

"Don't belittle yourself," said Thalkon, sincerely. "We told you the earth mind has the full *potential* of ours, if not the training. And you have just proved it. Now what we will do is return you to your cabin, where you will pretend to go about revealing to the world all about the Morlians *and* the Vigilantes…."

"I get it," said Thane. "As if I had broken with you in anger and just-wanted to inform my own people of what goes on. Then the Morlians won't suspect I'm still acting as your agent I can still put up my psycho-shield and fool them."

"Only now they will suspect psycho-tampering by us," warned Thalkon. "It will take infinite finesse."

"No, just human wits," said Thane, "which to them will be like animal cunning they don't understand. The ape can win, with luck—about a carload of it."

He turned to Miribel. "Well, sweet. Maybe this is goodbye…"

"Why?" she said. "I'm going along."

Thane and Thalkon stared at her.

"But Miribel—" they both began.

"Save your breath," the girl said firmly. "If Thane goes, I go. Besides, that will add to the deception, if I pretend—and I won't have to pretend—that I am madly in love with him and have deserted my people, and also want to expose the Morlian-Vigilante struggle to earth-people."

Thalkon's eyes gleamed. "Hmm. Twice in the past, Vigilantes who were agents on earth and mingled with earthpeople, fell in love. We had to kidnap the couple, in both cases, and return them to our world before they exposed us. The Morlians know the full story, so your act will seem quite true, Miribel. In a sense, it will cover up for Thane."

He turned and spoke into an intercom device. "Attention. Thane Smith and Miribel will be delivered to earth on Mission Main Base. Prepare a scout craft."

Before they left, Thalkon kissed Miribel lightly. "Good luck, daughter," he said.

"Daughter?" Thane stood stunned. "Why didn't you tell me before?" He recovered and went on, "And you're willing to risk your own daughter's life to help our world and defeat the Morlians."

It was not a question. Thane knew the answer already. The whole campaign of the Vigilantes was beyond the call of duty, protecting another world from some hideous fate.

Thane shook Thalkon's hand wordlessly, then stepped into the scout ship after Miribel. A computer might, in rigid objectivity, give zero odds that the three would ever meet again.

* * * *

"What are you doing?" asked Miribel curiously.

Thane looked up from his desk in the cabin, smiling. "I'm making out checks. One does have to pay bills, you know. Also I've got some correspondence to answer. If I don't somebody might get alarmed and tell the police I'm a missing man. That would mess up our plans but good."

Taking care of such routine affairs, Thane knew, was important, making it seem as if his life on earth was going on as usual. Otherwise, busybodies who suspected something was wrong might well raise a hue and cry and put him under an unwelcome spotlight.

Finally, heaving away from his desk with a sigh, Thane pointed at the typewriter and the girl sat down, poising her hands over the keys.

"Take this down, Miribel," said Thane, pacing up and down his cabin like a business executive. "I, Thane Smith, have absolute proof that extraterrestrial people have been visiting earth for at least 75 years. The proof? One of the extraterrestrials themselves, a girl named Miribel."

Out of the corner of his eye, Thane saw a domed saucer sliding down out of the sky and landing beyond a clump of trees. He knew the Morlian MIB's would quickly be on the job, keeping a sensor screen on the cabin day and night.

He went on dictating. "Miribel is the daughter of the Vigilante leader. His forces, in brief, are attempting to keep the Morlians—another alien race—from dominating earth."

Thane grinned to himself. Why they wanted to dominate earth, he did not know. The Vigilantes had never told him the it-is-not-permitted-to-tell secret. His ears now detected the soft pad of shoes outside.

"Miribel and I disagree with the Vigilante policy of secrecy and want the world to know the full story of why they and the Morlians are here…."

The door swung open. Three MIB's stalked in, tubular weapons in hand. "We would not like that," said their spokesman in typical mild tones.

"The Morlians," gasped Miribel in pretended surprise. "But you said your cabin would be safe, Thane."

"That's what I thought," said Thane, acting rueful.

"After I vanished so completely, I figured they would never check back here."

"You underestimate our thoroughness," said one MIB. "Now you will...."

They aimed their tubular weapons. Thane's heart froze. They were to be summarily killed after all, not captured. He had lost the big gamble at the start.

But only a soft hiss came from the devices and Thane felt his muscles go lax.

"...be paralyzed," finished the MIB, "and taken to our Supreme High, commander of all Morlians."

No, the gamble had won, exulted Thane. So far, at least.

The limp forms of Thane and Miribel were carried outside to the domed saucer, which moments later shot silently into the sky.

Destination—the unknown main base of Morli.

CHAPTER 19

Locked in a small chamber within the flying saucer, paralyzed but mentally alert, the captured pair had no idea of just where they were heading.

"It's not on earth," came Miribel's beamed psychowords, picked up by the psycho-wafer next to Thane's brain. "The departure mode was not an earthly trajectory but one out into space."

"At least we've eliminated one place where it is not," returned Thane, whimsically. "That leaves only eight other planets and thirty-odd moons. Not to mention 50,000 asteroids or so."

"Or maybe," speculated Miribel, "some artificial base in midspace, at any one of an infinite number of points near earth."

"Obviously," telepathed Thane, "we'll have to wait till we get there and then see where we are."

Their sense of time seemed dulled, too, by the induced paralysis. They had no idea if it was minutes or hours or days later when the saucercraft spun down for a landing.

A Morlian guard came in their prison chamber and shone the tubular device's ray at them, but this time with a different effect. Their muscles suddenly began working again.

"Follow me," he said tersely. Other guards fell in behind. They stepped from the saucer onto a railed catwalk within a giant dome.

Thane immediately knew, by how light he felt, that they were on some small body. The guard handed them each a pair of heavy metallic boots. "Put them on. They will hold you down. Otherwise you could not walk without bouncing around uncomfortably."

The boots, though not outsized, were extremely heavy. When Thane stood up, he felt as if only 50% earth-scale gravity were at work, which meant that this body was really small.

That eliminated all the planets and left their tiniest moons. Or an asteroid. But which one? The solid dome above had no skylight window to see the stairs. Thane ached to flash the big message to Thalkon, telling precisely where the Morlian headquarters were. When would they get the chance—if ever?

A flying platform, similar to those of the Vigilantes, took them through an arched entrance into an inner sanctum that was heavily guarded. Thane knew they were to confront the Supreme High, commander of multithousands of Morlian saucercraft and their crews.

In an austere chamber, a Morlian in a dead-black uniform sat in a throne-like onyx chair. He smiled genially as the two prisoners stood before him.

"Greetings, Thane Smith of earth," he said in a gentle voice that seemed to hold no hate or threat. "And Miribel of the Zyl Vigilantes."

The Supreme High picked up a document. "Thane Smith," he said in the same unreproachful tones, "you have proved our worst enemy, acting as a secret agent of the Vigilantes and causing the loss to us of ten bases in all. Do you deny it?"

It was hopeless to try. The Morlians were no fools and could add two and two. Thane shook his head. "Why were we brought here?" he asked, wanting to sound them out. "For execution?"

"No, not that," said the Morlian leader. "No, nothing as easy as that." His voice was not sadistic.

Thane and Miribel both squirmed inwardly.

"You are to undergo a certain mental procedure which will instantly leave you both idiots, drained of all mind-powers."

Mind dissection! Thalkon had guessed rightly. He glanced at Miribel. The horror in her eyes was of great magnitude.

"I will personally attend the test," said the Supreme High to his guards. "Yes, the great test!"

Test? Of what? Thane's wonder and dread grew as they were escorted into another great chamber. Most of it was taken up by a gigantic plastic box filled with countless rows of what looked like microminiaturized circuitry hung on vertical plates. All of it was immersed in some transparent viscous fluid.

"It reminds me of a computer," Thane said to Miribel.

"Or a giant battery," murmured the girl.

"You are both right," nodded the Supreme High, Who had come up behind them. "But a new kind of battery and computer never known before, with awesome powers—when it is done."

Miribel shuddered.

"I think the Zyl girl knows what is coming," said the Morlian chief, "Their spies gathered enough information in the past 75 earth years to piece together our final plan. And how earth fits into that plan."

Thane tensed. Was he about to hear from the Morlians themselves what Thalkon had refused to reveal?

But the Supreme High turned and beckoned to two chairs facing the huge machine. An inch-thick cable or tube led from each chair within the giant box.

"You will please be seated."

They both sat down. Thane suddenly felt himself gripped by an invisible force that emanated from the chair. Once seated, you could not get out though no bonds were visible. Some devilish Morlian device for holding you prisoner in front of the immense battery-computer.

"The test will be applied to the girl first," said the Supreme High. "Begin."

As the attendants used pushbuttons, a mirrored device descended from the ceiling until it hung just over Miribel's head. She glanced up, in frozen terror.

"Goodbye, Thane," she choked out.

It was all nightmarish after that, for Thane. He saw a purling blue ray shine down from the mirror, bathing Miribel's head. Her face distorted as if something were being torn from her. Thane strained against the invisible grip of his chair but could not move a muscle. He could only watch, in slowly growing horror.

"I will explain, earthman," came the voice of the Supreme High. "First of all, remember that a person s mind—the mentality or psyche—exists as an electromagnetic pattern independently of the physical brain. The brain, you see, is only an instrumented sensor of the true mind, lending it the senses of sight, hearing, tactility, and the rest."

Thane could dimly understand. At one time he had researched psychic phenomena which seemed to authenticate this fundamental separateness of mind and brain. Especially the so-called out-of-body experiences, in which a sensitive's 'astral' form left the physical body and wandered on its own, sometimes far across the world. It was the astral-form that held all the person's memory and awareness, while the deserted body lay inert, the brain uncomprehending. It was as if the mind had been 'drained' out of the brain, leaving it merely a blank mass of protoplasm.

"And Miribel's mind-psyche," said the Morlian chief with brutal directness, "is being *forced* out of her brain and is being drained away through that psychomagnetic cable."

Thane sickened as he saw the tubular cable form a bulge that slowly traversed its length and reached the giant box.

"Now," said the Supreme High, with a new tense note in his voice, "will her mind-psyche be successfully assimilated in that mind-battery?"

Mind-battery? A battery was something you poured energy into. Thane's mind screamed at the next thought that came to him. *Miribel's mind was being 'poured' into the giant box!*

Thane forced his eyes back to her face. He knew what he would see. It was a face of utter idiocy, grinning foolishly. Her eyes were vacant with no slightest sign of intelligence shining forth.

"Her brain," screeched Thane, squirming helplessly in his chair's grip. "You emptied her brain. Stop...stop..."

His voice broke to a bubbling moan.

"If the power needle swings up one notch," said the Supreme High, peering at a dial on the plastic box, "it will mean...ah!" His triumphant exclamation was almost a shout. "It worked. Miribel's full mentality is now available to the computer connected to the mind-battery."

"Horrible," Thane could only rasp, his whole being revolted at the ghoulish feat. "Miribel's mind gone, like a candle snuffed out. You turned her into a mindless nothing...mere living flesh...horrible, horrible. I loved her and she's gone...gone..."

"Oh, the process is reversible," said the Supreme High airily, waving a hand. Attendants worked controls and the bulge reappeared at the other end of the tube, leaving the mind-battery. When the bulge traveled to her chair, Miribel's drooling face began to change.

In a few moments, she turned and smiled faintly at Thane. "It wasn't goodbye after all," she breathed, but there was lurking horror in her eyes. "I felt myself...my mind...me...being drawn through the tube and into the plastic box. It felt like...no, I can't describe it." She broke off and shivered. Then she glanced in stark pity at Thane. "Now can you see what their plan is for earth?"

"No, I can't," mumbled Thane, still shaken by what had happened to her. "I don't want to know." He was fighting off any conjectures, afraid to face the mind-blasting denouement.

"But it was the finely tuned mind of Miribel of Zyl that we tested," the Morlian Chief was saying, turning his eyes balefully on Thane. "Now we must test the coarser mind of the earthling. Begin."

Thane braced himself as the mirror lowered over his head, still helpless to leap out of the chair and escape. At the purling blue ray's touch, infinite agony filled his head. He felt as if his brain were being ripped out. But he knew it wasn't his brain. It was his mind. The essence of his whole being. The true intangible *him*, an electromagnetic pattern stamped on his brain like the magnetic pattern on a voice-tape.

And his mind-psyche was being forced out of his brain and into the psychomagnetic tube. There was a soundless 'snap' and the pain ceased. He sensed that his mind-bulge was now traveling through the tube. It felt like going through a clammy cold tunnel into some impossible dimension.

Then he felt his mind-essence pouring into a receptacle in the plastic box, and being 'imprinted' therein. He was in the mind-battery. Dimly, his racing thoughts wondered if his mind would be returned to his body, like Miribel's. Or would he remain here, forever imprisoned within this horrifying psycho-battery like a charge of electricity?

But then he felt himself being drawn away, back through the tube. Moments later, with a soundless click, he was seeing with his eyes and hearing with his ears again.

"Again a complete success," said the Morlian chief tonelessly, though they were crowing words. "That means that M-day can be set for three days from now."

"M-day means *mind-day*," whispered Miribel to Thane, her voice edged with a moan.

"Our orbit will take us within 5000 miles of earth in three days," the Supreme High went on, speaking to his attendants more than to his prisoners. "From that close range, we can send the activator-signal to all our invisibly taped antennas planted on earth so laboriously in the past 75 years."

With dread clawing its way through him, Thane waited for the rest, not daring to consciously think ahead himself.

"Each antenna will then spread an umbrella of blue rays, completely covering earth's surface. The mind-psyches of all people on earth will then be forced out of their brains."

Thane winced violently with each statement after that.

"Our circling ships with psychomagnetic tubes lowered will suction up those loosened mind-psyches and keep them stored... Upon return to our main base here, the tubes will pour those captured human minds into the psycho-battery...."

"Fully charged, the psycho-battery will then feed mentality-units to the computer system...."

"And we will have a bio-computer of supercapacity, greater than any ever invented before in the universe, powered not by mere electronic impulses but by *three and a half billion human minds*."

Thane's mind flipped upside-down. He felt himself skirting the edges of insanity. A whole world—his world, "robbed" of 3½ billion mind-psyches—sent into mental slavery within a computing machine.

Now he knew why Thalkon had used 'ghastly' and 'fiendish' to describe the Morlian plot against the earth. But those words were too weak. There were no words to describe the supercrime that would be committed with multibillions of minds stolen from humanity on earth.

"With the mind-powered computer," the Supreme High was finishing, "we will of course be able to devise new ultraweapons far more powerful than those of the Vigilantes. Conquest of the universe will then follow with ease."

Thane knew he was not boasting. With 3½ billion mentalities given programmed instructions to work out the scientific and mathematical problems, they would be solved in billionths of a second. The output of this mind-powered computer would be inconceivably superior to any other computer known.

And the most grinding thought was that the stolen earth-minds would aid the empire-hungry Morlians in wrecking the United Worlds and sweeping through the galaxy as conquerors.

Maddening thought upon maddening thought. Miribel was staring pityingly at Thane. She shook her head, seeing him slowly go under.

"That is your punishment for the destruction of ten of our bases, Thane Smith," the Supreme High said. "Not to join your fellow people in the psycho-computer, but to live on and go mad when you are the only human left free."

The mildness of his tone, in contrast to his ruthless words, was far more blood-chilling than if he had roared in emotional theatrics.

"Release them from the chairs and imprison them together."

CHAPTER 20

For almost two days, Thane was a madman. Not a homicidal psychopath but a brooding wreck who moaned and groaned continuously, clenching and unclenching his fists helplessly. Miribel wept at the insane light in his tortured eyes.

How could any earthman withstand the stark and devastating picture of how his people—to the last man, woman, and child—would have body and mind shorn asunder, leaving 3½ billion breathing but mindless bodies to slowly die on earth like gross crawling slugs?

"That was why," Miribel murmured, "we did not want to tell you the Morlian earth-plot. That you heard it at all was the price you had to pay for aiding us as a spy. Poor Thane. Your mind will stay in your body—but hopelessly mad. And I loved you...."

She choked for a moment, then straightened up. A look of concentration came over her face as she began sending out a psycho-beam, contacting Thalkon. She told the grim story briefly.

"Then in one more day," returned Thalkon, "they will be within position to send the trigger-beam to their earth-based antennas and accomplish their aim—the theft of every mind on earth. Even if we attacked with all our forces at that time, their entire warfleet would be at hand, protecting the key-ship sending down the trigger beam and the mind-suction craft. We might wipe out most of their forces—and still lose. For they would have 3½ billion human minds safely stored in their psycho-battery, ready for use in the psycho-computer."

"The trouble is," Miribel said in frustration, "that we still don't know *where* this Morlian HQ is. We've had no chance to look out at the stars or at anything. And the psycho-beam between us is entirely non-directional. However, from the slight gravity, I suspect this is some very small asteroid."

"Fine," said Thalkon ironically. "Only 50,000 to choose from."

"No, not 50,000," came a new psycho-voice. "Just one."

Miribel turned with a little scream of joy. "Thane, it's you! Your eyes are clear. How—"

"I can't figure it out myself," said Thane wonderingly. "Unless everything that's happened to me in the past two weeks—seeing genuine saucers, the MIB's attacking, meeting the Vigilantes, hearing of the 75-year struggle, and all that—conditioned my mind to accept one more blow, the greatest of them all."

"What did you mean—one?" put in Thalkon tensely. "Which asteroid are you on, and how can you know?"

"Something stuck in my mind," said Thane slowly, "when the Supreme High said they would *orbit* close to earth in three days. Not long ago—when I was a disbeliever in UFO's—I wrote a science article about a sensational but unconfirmed observation made by a Japanese astronomer, claiming he had discovered a new eccentric asteroid. That was about six months ago."

Thane paused to sort his thoughts. "Eccentric asteroids are those that leave the main flock orbiting between Mars and Jupiter. These mavericks have crazy looping orbits that cross those of Mars and Venus. Icarus even crosses the orbit of Mercury and goes closer to the sun than any other body, except an occasional comet."

Thane lit a cigarette. "Some of these eccentric asteroids come fairly close to earth and are called *earth-grazers*, even though they may miss by four million miles or so. Eros is one, also Adonis and Apollo. Hermes came the nearest to earth in 1937, within 485,000 miles or just twice as far away as the moon."

After a hurried puff, Thane went on quickly. "But the Japanese astronomer was startled to find that his new eccentric earth-grazer would really graze earth—by 7500 miles. Now his hasty calculations, based on insufficient orbital data, could be wrong. The true figure might be *5000 miles*."

"The figure given by the Supreme High," breathed Miribel, excitedly. "Then it could be…"

Thalkon broke in urgently. "Can you remember any of the orbital data, Thane? If you give us any of the astronomer's figures, we can piece the rest out."

Thane furrowed his brow. "After all that has happened," he muttered half-complainingly, "anything that I wrote only a couple months ago seems so remote...hmm. I think I remember it was azimuth 43.6 degrees...uh...right ascension 11.4 degrees...and declination 65 point something. Latitude, Tokyo figure."

"And what was the date, Thane? That's all-important."

"The date?" Thane knocked knuckles at his temple in frustration. "You'd think I could remember a simple thing like that. But I'm blank...no, wait. I recall saying to myself that guy sure loves his job if he works on a holiday. But which holiday? Christmas?... July the Fourth?... Columbus Day?...aha! That's it. I remember saying to myself he's really celebrating Columbus Day by discovering a 'new world,' even if it was a tiny asteroid only 1/3 mile across. So that makes it..."

"October 12," supplied Miribel's psycho-voice. "We have studied your earthly calendar and important dates."

"That's it, Thane. The downfall of Morli—if we hurry."

Thalkon's psycho-voice became hesitant as he continued. "I'm sorry to say this but there is no choice. You have 24 hours to escape from the asteroid. Then it will be blown up. Good luck, Thane... and daughter."

His psycho-voice faded out. Thane and the girl stared at each other.

"24 hours to escape," mumbled the girl, "from the enemy's main armed camp, while locked up in a dome. It's impossible."

"It's only the miraculous that gives us trouble," said Thane with an attempt at lightness. "The impossible we do with ease."

But he wasn't fooling the girl—or himself.

Thane was too tired to think. He swayed on his feet, bone-weary from his two days of sleepless madness.

"Got to have a nap," he muttered, stumbling toward one of the two cots in the corner of the room.

Miribel was equally in need of rest and fell onto the other cot. And so, with only 24 hours left before the deadline of doom, the two slept half of it away.

Miribel awoke first and shook Thane until he opened his eyes droopily. "We have an inner 'clock' or time-sense. We've slept 12 horns. In 12 more hours the Vigilante fleets will be here to blast the asteroid to bits."

"Twelve horns to escape—and I still haven't a plan." Thane began pacing the floor, trying to think a way out of their dilemma. He stopped in midstride, staring down at the bulky shoes they had been supplied with.

"Miribel, did they feed us during the past two days when I was…uh…out of my head?"

"Yes, Thane. Two guards, heavily armed, came in twice a day with food. They probably came while we were asleep too, but left without awakening us."

"Does your time-sense tell you when they are due again?" Thane demanded tensely.

"Hmm…I would say in about four hours."

"Four wasted hours," said Thane in the tones of a curse. "But anyway, we can go over a plan to overcome the two guards. How were they armed?"

"Each with two weapons at his hip—a blaster and a para-gun that shoots the paralyzer-ray."

"Did both men come in?"

"No," said the girl. "One came in with the food while the other stood just outside the door, ready to use his guns if need be. And how can we overcome them?"

"With these," said Thane. He held up one of his weighted shoes which he had removed, but only with an effort. He dropped the shoe. It struck the floor with a heavy thud. "How do they make them ten times heavier than lead?" he wondered.

"Atom-packing," said Miribel. "The metal is placed in a powerful force field that constricts at the center. The atoms are simply crushed together until their specific density is 10 times greater than before."

Another sign of the advanced science-technology the saucer-men—whether Vigilantes or Morlians—had brought with them. Thane smiled grimly. "We'll turn their own technology against them, in this particular case. Now here is how we'll work it, when the guards come…"

Miribel listened intently and gave a few suggestions of her own.

The door swung open after being unlocked and the guard came in, balancing a tray of dishes. The second guard stood watchfully in the doorway.

"Your food," said the first guard, glancing at the two prisoners, who sat on their cots as if just awakening. Their blankets had fallen carelessly around their feet.

As the guard stooped to set the tray down on the central table, Miribel suddenly yanked something from under her blanket. Using two hands to lift her heavy shoe, she brought it down on the guard's head. He sank without a sound.

The other guard at the door immediately began tugging at the two weapons slung in his belt. But almost at the same time Miribel had used her shoe, Thane had yanked one of his shoes from under his blanket and flung it toward the doorway.

The guard dodged it, but this threw off his aim as he fired his para-gun. And before he could fire again, Thane's second shoe smacked straight into his face. With a grunt the guard keeled over.

"Out cold," gloated Thane, running over, "as if he had been slugged by the world's champion heavyweight fighter. Those weighted shoes pack a punch."

Thane dragged the second guard alongside the first guard. Quickly, he took all four of their weapons. He handed the two para-guns to Miribel, tucking the two blasters in his own belt.

"Now for step two," breathed Thane, "according to our plan. We have to make our way out of these sleeping quarters—our prison was only a spare bunkroom—to the spaceship hangar. And as you surmise, from your knowledge of Morlian architecture, that would be at the far end of the dome. And this is a big dome, maybe a mile wide."

It seemed almost foolish to try, with innumerable guards between them and their objective. Thane cautiously led the way out of their prison room, closing the door behind them.

They were wearing their weighted shoes again and walked normally down the hallway. At the end of the corridor, where a doorway opened out into the main section of the dome, a guard stood with his back to them.

Silently taking off one shoe, Thane crept up behind him and laid him out with one sweeping blow. "Great weapons, these shoes," whispered Thane. "Too bad we can't take them along."

Shoeless, they slipped out of the doorway. Around them now as the full sweep of the gigantic dome, its top barely visible. Dotted here and there were other barracks buildings, laboratories, workshops arsenals, and all the installations of a warbase.

Dimly, at the far side of the dome, they could see a huge hangar where the Morlian warfleets and scout craft lay. Between them and their goal stood thousands of Morlians.

"All of whom we skip meeting," grinned Thane, taking the girl's hand. "Now.... JUMP."

They jumped straight up. Without the weighted shoes, in the almost negligible gravity of the tiny asteroid, they kept going up—50 feet...a hundred...two hundred. At 500 feet, still sailing up in a currying trajectory, Thane grabbed hold of a girder and clung to it. With his other hand, he easily swung a one-pound Miribel up onto the metal beam.

Thane looked around. They were on one of the spidery network of beams supporting the domed structure. Not a great deal of bracing was needed in this low gravity. The beam was no more than 6 inches wide and an inch thick. On earth or any other planet or moon, these thin girders would have collapsed in seconds.

"Now we simply follow this 'pathway,' 500 feet high, to the other side of the dome," Thane said exultantly.

"A stroke of genius, that idea," said Miribel admiringly. "The moment you mentioned it, I realized we had some chance."

Toning down their leg muscles, they minced their way along the girder to where it joined other girders at the center of the dome, all affixed to a single pillar. Then they strode along another branching girder that led toward the hangar a half-mile away.

"Nobody will think of looking up here for us," said Thane. "But move slowly so that if any Morlian accidentally glances up and spies us, he won't be sure—at that distance—whether his eyes are playing him tricks or not."

Fortunately, the dome's lighting facilities consisted of a series of luminescent fixtures hanging from the girder system and shining their light downward only. The upper part of the dome, where the two escapees crawled along, was in comparative gloom.

When they reached a position directly over the hanger, Thane halted. "How many hours left before the big blast?"

"Seven," returned Miribel. "By now, the Vigilante astronomical experts must have calculated just where this asteroid is located in space, from the data you gave. Thalkon has probably already given the order for all warfleets to prepare for action at zero-hour. They are on their way now, from all bases in the solar system."

A ring of deadly ships closing in on the lone asteroid, ready to blast it to eternity—in seven hours. Thane shivered.

He glanced down. There was the usual bustle and activity below, within and outside of the hanger—mechanics, pilots, workmen and all others, doing their duties. At times a scout ship took off and shot straight up to the dome's peak, there turning half-transparent and 'oozing' out through the solid wall. Thane could still not get over the wonder of it, since experiencing it at the sea dome.

"Are you sure," fretted Thane, "that the Morlians have a waking and sleeping period, like on earth?"

"Yes," nodded Miribel. "They are creatures of habit, as all intelligent beings seem to be throughout the galaxy."

"And when will their sleep period come?"

"In five hours, at the soonest." The girl looked gravely at Thane. "Or as long as 8 hours, if my estimates are wrong."

"Eight hours," grunted Thane, turning a little pale. "We'll never live that long. It's got to come before seven hours…or else."

CHAPTER 21

Time did not drag. It fairly flew. Three hours passed and Thane could picture the Vigilante armada gathering speed and plunging through space toward a tiny spark in space that was nearing earth, ready to graze it by 5000 miles.

Thane could also picture the Supreme High, chief of the Morlians, gloatingly watching earth enlarge with his finger poised at the button that would trigger off instant doom for all earth-people.

Four hours passed…five hours.

"Two more hours to go," whispered Miribel.

"And still no sign of any slackening off below," groaned Thane. "Our only hope is to steal one of their ships, but not while a thousand Morlians are around. When will they ever knock off work and…"

"Wait," said Miribel sharply. "They won't. Oh, Thane, it was stupid of me. But you see, they won't stop working today. They will be sending out all or most ships to carry out the earth-doom project in two hours."

"That's right," gasped Thane with a sinking heart. "All their ships equipped with the mind-suction tubes and military escorts."

And just then, taking off one by one, a hundred huge saucer-craft spun out of the hangar and out of the dome.

"The same thing is happening at perhaps a dozen other domes on the asteroid," surmised Miribel. "All their vast fleet will be poured into this giant operation."

In the next hour, another thousand craft silently poured out of the hangar and out of the dome, for their rendezvous with—earth.

Suddenly, a psycho-voice boomed in their minds. "Thalkon calling Thane Smith and Miribel. The Supreme High, we calculated, would set his zero-hour for the moment when the asteroid is closest to earth—two hours from now. We will strike one hour from now. It was the best we could do, as to timing." He seemed to draw a breath. "Now, have you any chance of escaping before the end?"

Thane glanced at the girl's taut face. "It's going to be touch-and-go, Thalkon. But of course, nothing must hold up your attack at the specified time. If we lose out, only two lives are lost. If you lose out, 3½ billion lives are lost—on earth."

"Goodbye, father," said Miribel's psycho-voice resignedly, "in case we never see you again."

"May the Great Guardian bless you both for what you have done, making our victory possible."

His psycho-voice faded out.

"Come on," snapped Thane. "I'll be damned if I'll sit here and wait for the axe to fall. Down we go, depending on the element of surprise to carry us through."

With that, Thane made a swan-dive off the girder, Miribel instantly following. They glided down in slow-motion, with no danger of landing with killing shock.

They landed on the roof of the hangar. A quick look around and he pointed at a cupola. "An air duct, as I hoped. Let's go."

They wormed their way into the air duct, then hung over the scene of activity, as more Morlian saucercraft wheeled out.

"Drop down on that one below, in back of those now leaving," hissed Thane. "If we're in luck, the pilot or pilots will be too busy with their instruments to see us." Their two featherweight bodies drifted down toward the domed disk below. Their feet hardly made a sound as they landed. Miribel pointed silently at the open hatchway in the side of the dome.

As they crept, they came face to face with a startled Morlian pilot, about to close the hatch.

Thane had one of his blasters in hand, but hesitated. Unlike a Vigilante weapon, it would not hurl the victim into the Nth dimension, but into oblivion. Thane sweated....

But Miribel's para-gun was already hissing and the Morlian pilot slumped like a rag doll.

"Good work," said Thane thankfully.

He dragged him across the saucer's rounded top to the rim and dropped him off. Leaping headlong in a fifty-foot dive back to where Miribel stood, Thane led the way inside the saucer.

"If the other pilot heard anything, he'll be coming to investigate," whispered Miribel. "Listen…his footsteps."

They sounded from a cross corridor that came from the pilot's bubble. Thane got down in a ready crouch. It would be too risky trying to gun him down from a distance. As soon as the Morlian turned the corner, Thane leaped, hurling his body 30 feet down the corridor. The impetus of his earth muscles shot him forward like a cannon shell. His head struck the Morlian in the chest, thrusting him backward for 10 feet, meeting a wall with a sodden thud.

"Two down," panted Thane, "and none to go. Hurry, to the pilot room."

In the pilot's bubble of transparent material, they sat down at the controls. "Can you drive this crate, Miribel?" At the girl's nod, Thane went on. "You take the drive controls. I'll take the gun controls, of the second seat. Tell me how they work."

Miribel ran through it swiftly, Thane nodding and absorbing it. "Now, the trick is…"

A radio voice broke in from their panel speaker, in an alien gibberish.

"The Morlian language," said Miribel. "I'll translate… *Blaster craft #Z-777. Prepare for take-off. Follow route ZY. That is all.*"

Faking a man's gruff voice, Miribel then spoke into a panel mike, and Thane assumed she gave the Morlian equivalent of 'Roger.' She shut off the mike carefully, then worked pushbuttons that made their saucer trundle itself out of the hangar on wheels. Outside, she retracted the wheels and began to spiral the saucer upward in the same take-off pattern the preceding ship had used.

"If nobody caught a glimpse of us in our bubble," Thane breathed, "we have a good chance to get away scot free. How much time to the deadline, Miribel?"

"Just twenty minutes."

"Ouch," said Thane with a world of feeling. "If anything delays us…"

"We re gone gooses," said Miribel, unconsciously using earth idiom. They smiled bleakly at each other.

Miribel expertly used the off-phase control to shift their vibrational range to where they could ooze through the solid dome into open space. At that moment, the automatic speaker circuit boomed out ominously.

"Attention!" translated Miribel. "Emergency alarm! Two unauthorized persons have been seen in ship #Z-777. Chase them down, if you are near."

She turned to Thane, face ashen. "That's our fatal delay," Miribel said, pointing to where three Morlian saucers were wheeling around and coming at them.

"Not if I work fast—and you outmaneuver them," hissed Thane. "Come on, give me the right shooting positions."

The Morlian ships were already hurling out blaster-beams, but Miribel played her fingers dancingly over the control keyboard, and their saucer slewed away at a right angle.

Thane again marveled, in flashing thought, at the miraculous null-inertia system that allowed these saucers to turn and twist in violent flying contortions without straining one bolt. Miribel's fingers kept playing a skillful tattoo and their saucer spun crazily, or so it seemed. But suddenly she yelled: "Now, Thane!"

And Thane found he had a perfect shot at the backside of one Morlian saucer. Pressing the stud of his blast-gun, Thane sent one vicious blaster-beam stabbing ahead. The enemy craft burst into a billion sparkles, just as the first saucer had dining the dogfight on earth that he had witnessed.

Morlian blast-beams narrowly missed them in the next minute. But twice more Miribel wrenched their ship through impossible turns to utterly surprise the Morlian pilots. And twice more Thane had the satisfaction of seeing space fireworks herald the end of Morlian war-craft.

"Unfortunately, we are forced to take Morlian lives," said Miribel, with a pained face. "They never equipped their weapons to send out the saving ray that first hurls a living pilot to the Nth dimension before his ship blows up."

"That was only three Morlian lives," spat out Thane without remorse. "They were ready to wipe out all humanity…."

"Look!" yelled Miribel. "We've got to get out of here fast. There comes the Vigilante warfleet."

Thane stared. A cloud in space was expanding and blocking out the stars. The cloud grew immense as a vast fleet of Vigilante ships arrowed toward the asteroid on which lay a dozen domes.

Miribel worked frantically at her controls trying to slew their saucer out of the path of the growing cloud. But the cloud expanded faster than their flight path.

"Hopeless," said Miribel tightly. "The Vigilante fleet probably covers an area of space a million miles wide. It's like a bug trying to escape a vast flock of birds."

"And we're in a Morlian ship—which they'll shoot down," added Thane. "We escaped the asteroid but not soon enough."

"We're sitting ducks, as you would say on earth."

"But we're not through," protested Thane. "We simply contact Thalkon with a psycho-beam."

He tried. Miribel tried. There was no answer. "We can't get through to him," Miribel said tonelessly. "I didn't expect to. As commander of this all-out attack against the main Morlian base, he's receiving hundreds of psycho-messages from his subcommanders."

"And ours is lost in the shuffle," said Thane. "But we're going to make our death count. Swing back, Miribel. Back to where the Morlian fleet is massing. Get it? They won't know it's us. We'll be right in the middle of their fleet and then open up on all sides." His face was savage now.

Their saucer spun in a long arc to join the outer fringes of the Morlian fleet. The ships originally sent toward earth had been hastily recalled when the approaching Vigilante fleet had been detected.

But it was a haphazard formation and in the disorder, Miribel weaved her ship toward the central core. They did not have long to wait.

With the arrival of the Vigilante vanguard, both sides opened fire. Fission and fusion powered, a wide assortment of blast-beams stabbed back and forth. Morlian ships began to burst into brilliant showers of sparks. But the rest had formed roughly into a phalanx in depth, in the path of the Vigilante armada.

"Now's the time," hissed Thane. "We'll punch a hole through them for the Vigilante fleet to get through."

Thane's finger went down on the filing button. A livid blast-beam caught the nearest Morlian ship squarely, creating another sunburst of sparks in space. As Miribel swung the ship around slowly, Thane fired continuously, raking Morlian craft like a row of targets in a shooting gallery.

"They don't know what hit them," gloated Thane, then kept up the grim count he had begun "...25...26...27...28..."

Utterly bewildered at the attack, the Morlian formation began to break up ahead. Two craft even rammed each other in the confusion.

Thane laughed aloud and counted mentally. "...46...47...48..."

CHAPTER 22

Miribel glanced back and gasped.

"Thane! Where *is* the asteroid?"

Thane whirled. There was no asteroid back of them, as there should be. Then, in the corner of his eye, he caught sight of the small dim body, slowly receding into space.

"It's *moving*," said Thane, stunned. "The Supreme High had an ace up his sleeve. The asteroid is powered somehow."

Miribel groaned audibly. "And if the Morlian fleet holds up the Vigilante forces long enough, the Supreme High can slip close to earth, send out the ships with psycho-suction tubes, and steal all earthy minds. Then he could lose himself and his tiny asteroid in space. Under power, he would return safely to Morli with his psychobattery fully 'charged' to operate his psycho-computer and plot the conquest of the cosmos."

"Damn," swore Thane in a rage, "how can we stop him? Wait, what power system would the asteroid have?"

"I can only guess," said Miribel slowly, swinging their saucer around to follow the receding asteroid. "It would have to be an electrogravity power plant, such as the kind the United Worlds Planetary Engineering Bureau uses for moving moons around and reshaping solar systems that are badly arranged by nature."

"Where would it be located?" Thane asked hurriedly.

"Probably under an aerated dome for the benefit of the engine crew. The telltale sign would be an aura of violet light around it, a standard by-product of the electrogravity power plant."

"Then catch up with the asteroid," snapped Thane. He grinned crookedly. "They'll take our saucer for one of their own, returning from some military mission or other. With the emergency at hand, it's a sure thing nobody will be watching every ship that comes down." Miribel nodded and rammed the saucer ahead, soon overtaking the runaway asteroid. Beyond, earth was ballooning into a ball that rapidly enlarged. Calculating rapidly, Miribel warned: "Thane! The asteroid will be within 5000 miles of earth in just 5 minutes."

"Unless we find the right dome and stop it," supplied Thane, peering down intently as they swooped low over the asteroids jagged surface. Three domes appeared, widely spaced. None of them glowed with violet light.

"The next dome, Miribel," fumed Thane. "Hurry!"

More minutes were wasted in checking nine more domes. Then Thane stared below at the first dome they had seen hove into view. "No more domes?" he gasped.

Miribel shook her head. "I circled the asteroid in an orbital pattern, shifting each time and covering the whole surface. They have only 12 domes." Her voice was edged with panic. "Did I guess all wrong about an electrogravity power plant? Thane, the Supreme High's zero-moment is close now. Only a minute left…."

Thane stiffened and pointed down. "Look. A violet glow from that miniature mountain peak."

Miribel stared eagerly, her face lighting up. "They *camouflaged* it under stone. Get ready, Thane. As I make a low pass over the peak, send down an infra melt-beam. Fourth button to the right on your weapon keyboard."

The saucer tilted and sliced downward at a steep slant. As it abruptly made a 60-degree turn just above the mountain, an angry red beam spat forth and touched the peak. Molten lava instantly formed as the peak melted away.

"Now to get away fast," Miribel half-screeched, sending their saucer careening away at 1000-g's of acceleration. "When that molten stone floods down into the power plant and wrecks the electrogravity unit, at least 100 giga-dynes will be released."

Dynes? Dynes? Then Thane remembered. The unit of energy. And "giga" was the metric system's prefix for "billion."

The asteroid had receded behind them to a tiny star. But suddenly the star grew into a nova, then a supernova. And still it grew and grew and grew….

An invisible tide of smashed molecules, driven at superhurricane speed, overtook the fleeing saucer. The blow was like that of a giant fist, tumbling the saucer like a cork. Inside, Thane was thrown against the side wall with a shade less than bone-crushing force. Then Miribel's flying form struck him in the chest, knocking his breath out explosively.

Cushioned from a crash into metal by Thane's body, the girl recovered first, whimpering as a dozen bruises throbbed painfully. Thane lay sprawled on the floor, limp, pale, not breathing. Miribel felt for his pulse.

"Dead," she said hollowly.

* * * *

Thane sat up. He was in a white-walled chamber, in bed. Obviously a Vigilante sick bay aboard one of their ships. The door opened and Miribel came in, followed by Thalkon.

"I'm alive?" marveled Thane, feeling himself all over. "But I was sure I was dying, back in the Morlian saucer…."

"You did die," said Miribel matter-of-factly.

Thane grunted. "All right, what's the punch line?"

"It is not a joke," spoke up Thalkon, smiling. "Miribel rushed you here to my flagship. We didn't shoot down her Morlian ship because the battle was over and all Morlians were surrendering. Our doctors then restarted your heart electrically, used a bio-bellows to get your lungs pumping, and gave drugs that revved up your other organs."

Thane arched his brow. "On earth, I'd have been in a funeral parlor, being fixed up for my grand exit from this world."

"Our medical science is a bit ahead of yours," said Thalkon in an enormous understatement.

"The asteroid…?"

"Scattered through the solar system as atomic debris," said Thalkon. "The Supreme High never sent down the trigger-beam for his great mental thievery—thanks to you and my daughter. It was a magnificent feat."

Miribel didn't blush, but Thane did.

"With the explosion of their asteroid, and all their plans, the Morlians lost all heart to continue the pointless battle. They surrendered. We captured 40,000 craft. Their crews will be sent to exile in the Nth Dimension." He drew up, pointing at the globe of earth in space. After 75 years of struggle, your world is free of menace… until the next time."

"Thanks to *you* and the Vigilantes," said Thane earnestly.

Thalkon shrugged. "It's our duty." He eyed Thane speculatively. "Now the question is, what to do with you. You're the only earthman who knows all about the flying saucers. The tremendous earth-shaking truth. But we request—"

"I know, I know," said Thane. "You request that I never reveal this to anyone on earth. I promise."

"That may not be good enough," said Thalkon half-apologetically, "human nature being what it is. So—"

He took a medallion out of his pocket and held it before Thane's eyes. HONORARY MEMBER, GALACTIC VIGILANTE CORPS, SOL-EARTH SPECIAL AGENT.

"—we invite you into our ranks, sealing your lips according to our code. Do you accept, Thane Smith?"

"I'm honored," said Thane simply and sincerely. "But do I have any…well, actual duties as a 'special agent,' whatever that means?"

"It means you will be called upon by us, whenever necessary, in case earth becomes the target of a new menace. The defeat of Morli will leave a vacuum here. Other predatory worlds may step in. What your duties will then be, we cannot foretell."

He waved a hand. "But otherwise, you will simply resume your earth life, as before—with one change. You will have a wife. That is, after you're duly married in the earthly style."

Miribel still did not blush but stared back at Thane boldly. "Yes, I asked for earth duty along with you, Thane." Then suddenly she was shy. "You of course have the right to refuse."

"I accept," grinned Thane, "Mrs. Miribel Smith-to-be."

* * * *

"Listen to this TV news item, dear," called Thane. "For laughs."

Miribel came in from the kitchen, wiping her hands. On the screen, a news commentator told of a new sighting. A switch to videotape showed the witness, a respected professor, who recounted his story.

"It was a dancing light in the sky at first, coming down. It seemed about to crash to earth. Amazingly, however, it came to a dead halt 500 feet over me. Then I could clearly distinguish its shape, similar to two pie-plates placed together. Definitely metallic and powered. Definitely a machine."

The commentator came on again, a slight smile quivering at his lips, as he introduced the next videotape guest, a member of Air Force's Blue Book Staff.

The well-groomed officer who appeared spoke emotionlessly, without a hint of sarcasm. "After thorough study, and consultation with dozens of scientific experts, we have come to the conclusion that the professor was unknowingly deceived. It was the planet Venus that he saw, low over the horizon, where the refraction of the atmosphere can distort its image into many queer shapes—such as that of a flying saucer."

The officer stared out at the audience, his well-schooled face under control: "The Air Force wishes to emphasize again that there is no evidence whatsoever that UFO's, or flying saucers, are real objects, ships from other worlds driven by extraterrestrial beings, exist. Thank you."

"That," sighed Thane, "is where I came in." He turned to look out the window. The world beyond lay in total ignorance. "It's a pretty lonely feeling, being the only man on earth who knows the truth...."